I0636064

Hidden Secrets

Hidden Secrets

❧

Tapping into Your Emotional, Spiritual and Sexual Appetite to Win in Relationships

Ramon Darnell

Earthquake Publications
Chicago, IL ©2021
ISBN: 9780999221310

Table of Contents

Acknowledgements

I want to thank my team for all their hard work, with a special shout out to the leader of my team. You all know who you are. Thank you to my editor-extraordinaire who I adore.

For all my readers looking for that pot of gold, this is for you!

This is a work of creative fiction. Any resemblance to an actual person living or deceased, actual events in history, are purely coincidental.

Introduction

You might ask why I'm writing a book about this topic? What makes you an expert on relationships? Sometimes you are born with knowledge about things and sometimes you have experience about other things. I have both.

As a man I have had over 400 hundred relationships and have worked in the hair industry for over 25 years. As a salon owner and hair stylist, I worked with individuals from all walks of life. The hairstylist is like the bartender—you hear it all. I have talked to many women that have been in relationships that discussed various issues and problems with me about the male/female dynamic. What I noticed most consistently is there was, and is, a definite disconnect between males and females, and I knew from my years of experience that I had the insight to help solve this problem.

In other words, it ain't nothing but a chicken wing on a string—something simple as a nursery rhyme; winner, winner chicken dinner. It is just that easy.

One day one, of my faithful clients came to me for advice regarding her marriage. She started to tell me that she had found her husband of 7 years in their bed with another woman. She was devastated and broken by this. She felt they were in a good place after 7 years of marriage and was so confused by why he would do such a thing to hurt her so. She asked me what she should do.

This story is one of many that I intend to tell in this book. As a reformed player, hairstylist, and as a friend to numerous females over the years, there is nothing regarding relationships I have not heard. As for this specific story, we will revisit it later in the book and what I told her and how this problem was resolved.

The hairstylist is like the bartender, and the salon is like the therapy chair…

Prologue

BEFORE I OPENED my eyes, I could hear the TV and the news reporting that it was going to be a very bad thunderstorm. That seemed to drain all the energy out of me. I put the cover over my head and tried to think of any excuse not to get out of bed, less known to do anybody's hair on this gloomy September morning. Nevertheless, my die-hard customers would do anything to get their hair done. It would have to be a category 5 hurricane or some type of natural catastrophe to keep them away. I counted to three, pulled the covers back, and stretched and caught a glimpse of myself in the mirror, and pulled my curly hair into a ponytail. I brushed my teeth for 15 minutes and flexed my biceps and my six-pack, and jumped in the shower. I cooked my highly nutritional breakfast of boiled turkey, organic oatmeal, and an egg white omelet with mushrooms, spinach, and avocado. I lazily got myself together, walked out the door, and as a breeze hit my face, it woke me up a little bit more. Then I hopped in the car and drove to the salon. I was thinking to myself, *I can't wait to see who is going to show up in this type of weather.*

I turned into the parking lot, and it was not full. As I eased out of the car, the thunder rumbled. That put some pep in my step toward the door. A couple of raindrops hit my face while pulling the door open. They don't call it the Windy City for nothing as the wind swirled around me as I pushed my way into the salon.

Zsa Zsa, one of my long-time, loyal clients, followed me impatiently with her eyes as I slowly glided with a cool stroll to my station, taking my time.

She snarled. "You're late, Casanova!" as I turned toward her.

"I know. The early bird gets the goodies, right?" I answered.

"Ramon, you need to go to bed earlier and stop having those multiple rendezvous every night."

I looked around the salon, and only 4 girls had shown up out of the stylists that worked there. As I pulled out my cape and draped it over Zsa Zsa, I could see the reception desk at the front of the salon was still empty, and there were four clients waiting in the black chairs in the waiting area. The mirrors surrounding each station were squeaky clean, with each station having lime green chairs, and the stations surrounded the lime green dryers that were lined up in the middle of the salon.

My attention was drawn toward the front as I heard pounding footsteps moving quickly toward the door. The door swung open, and you could feel a gust of wind rush in as the first of my crew arrived, and my one and only receptionist, Sweet Pea, sashayed in.

Sweet Pea was 45 with skin that reminded you of sweet chocolate, 5'9, tall, lean with nice hips and feline eyes. She always wore her clothes well; fashionable and classy was the only way to describe her unique style. Larger than life presence but very narrow-minded, she was constantly controlled by her emotions. Her motto was if it did not feel good in her mind, it was wrong. On the flip side, she was highly social, a great conversationalist with a tender side. She could be very warm and sensitive.

"I had to hurry up. It had started to rain, and brown sugar melts when it gets wet," she said with a sexy grin.

A few seconds later, my girl Guru came in.

"What's the deal, Great One?

"It's all about the Roller Disco, baby!" I replied,

Great One was a nickname they called me because of my great skills at handling hair. Guru was 40 with dark velvet smooth skin, 5'3, with a voluptuous curvy figure, beautiful white teeth, and comforting eyes. She was always well put together and an extremely skilled hairstylist. She experienced two failed marriages. She married at an early age because she fell madly in love. The second marriage was her forever marriage. She believed this one would stand the test of time. To her surprise, it failed, and now she was exploring why it hadn't worked. Guru was seeking to discover who she really was and what she really wanted in a relationship.

Sunshine walked in with her high energy smile.

"What's going on, everybody?" she said.

She did natural hair. Sunshine was 47 with a peanut butter complexion, 5'4, slim but not skinny, well proportioned, dark brown, naturally curly hair, casual dress, round, soulful eyes with a warm sparkle. She was slightly militant. When provoked, she could become extremely emotional. Married for 20 years but bent a few curves in her young heyday that balanced her out well. This balance of emotions made her diplomatic, approachable, domestic, and it showed in her attitude when she communicated.

Mini and Boonie trotted in together one on the heel of the other.

Mini was overly polite. Everything sounded like an introduction as she said, "Hello, Everyone."

She was 35 with a paper bag brown skin tone, short, wavy golden blond hair, 5' 6, with big breasts, thick legs, and a huge butt. Her specialty was short hair, and she consistently wore her favorite color—black. She had piercing eyes that could cut you to the core. She was a bundle of passion and emotion, but when she used it wrong, it was detrimental. She was the epitome of feminist power, intellectual and graceful. She embraces other women, clings to their pain because of her hatred of men, which created her own underlying issues. She is sexually repressed due to this.

Boonie said, "Yo, Yo!"

She was always a shade too loud and an expert colorist. Boonie was 39 with dark brown skin, 5'7, black hair tapered close on the sides and back, large twinkling eyes, thick lips with a girlish smile. She had a robust figure, neat and conservative; a social butterfly that knows how to work a room. Fun-loving, happy-go-lucky, but very analytical. She has two sides; she uses her past hurts of molestation to fuel her rage against men, which is the temperature gage to her reaction to male/female problems. If a man gets into a compromising situation, she will never give him the benefit of the doubt. The only man different from all other men is her God-sent husband. Her better half is a tamed Beta male.

Camelot eased in with a subtle, "Hey."

Camelot was good with weaves and lace fronts. Camelot was 30, caramel-skinned, 5' 2", medium build. She frequently changed the color of her hair. Some days it was black, some days red, some days blonde. Everything she wore was tight-fitting to display every curve of her body. Her pants were so tight you could see her camel toe, which is why we called her Camelot. She had brown almond-shaped eyes with a very lustful glare. Her mouth was bow-shaped, and she liked to wear cherry red lipstick. With her baby doll looks, it was obvious she fed off attention. She made certain in some capricious way for everyone to know she was in the building. Very impulsive, a risk-taker, refused to accept no for an answer and could become aggressive. It was cool to notice her, but if you gave her an inch, she would take a mile.

As I put a towel around my client's neck, getting her prepared for a shampoo, Zsa Zsa spoke out. "Hey, Camelot. Girl, those pants are on fire! You look hot! Those black patent leather pants are dripping off of you!" Zsa Zsa was older and hung out with an older crew. She was all about women's power, but Camelot was a lot younger. They may not have understood each other at times—some wires could get crossed.

"Hey Zsa, don't keep complimenting her so hard! She likes girls," I said.

"Oh, she's cool. She won't take it wrong. When I was younger, you should have seen me. I was 36 24 46 what you talking about! Man, I had the most sculpted butt. My butt was so sculpted all the men did a double-take," Zsa said and repeatedly complimented Camelot.

Camelot shot right up to her like a Spike Lee movie about 2 inches from Zsa's face, licking her lips like she was hungry, and said, "You like this? What do you like about this?"

Zsa looked up into the air and shifted her eyes from side to side as a sound came from her. "Hummunah Hummunah Hummunah".

"Don't play with me," Camelot said as she rolled her eyes and backed slowly away to her station. You could stick a fork in Zsa. She was done.

It was ironic. I was the only man in the salon, but I loved all the ladies I worked with. It was a good thing most of my crew was in the house. I gave them all certain nicknames— Sweet Pea, Guru, Sunshine, Mini, Boonie, and Camelot to solidify my allegiance that they were all my favorites. Sweet Pea went over to the coffee maker and started the morning coffee. I could soon smell the fresh aroma of percolating coffee.

Mini announced to the ladies, "We got donuts, everybody!"

"I don't really eat a lot of sugar," one client said, but her feet were moving in that direction. All the sugar fanatics could not wait to get their sugar fix for the day.

Mini opened the blinds, so we could keep track of the storm as we worked diligently trying to accommodate all the clients before the storm got any worse. We finished up in a timely manner, working like eager beavers. No sooner had we let out the last customer then the sky lit up with lightning. We heard the roar of thunder, and the clouds opened up, and water poured out of them ferociously. We knew then that we would not be going home anytime soon.

Sweet Pea walked to the front door and gazed out at the huge raindrops plopping on the sidewalk. "There are two things I hate, big wind and thunderstorms."

Sunshine walked over to the chair at her station and slouched down, and said, "All storms ain't bad. That's love making weather!"

"Yeah, you got a husband," Guru chimed in. "I need to curl up with some biceps and triceps so I can enjoy this storm."

"There is definitely some joy in a storm. It relieves you of your duties. No one expects you to do anything. You can just chill," I replied

"I had a bad experience with rain, so I don't like to go out when it is raining. But it does help me to sleep. If my husband wants to get freaky deaky during a storm, he can get it!" Boonie said

"The only thing I see rain good for is to replenish the earth with fruits and vegetables," Mini interjected.

"You all are getting too philosophical about this. I was just talking about the natural occurrence between a man and a woman that can be very fulfilling during a storm," Sunshine said.

I stood up, walked around my chair, and said, "You are supposed to plant seeds and be fruitful in whatever you do, ladies. That's what life is all about. Even in relationships, even when it comes to men and women. If you plant good seeds, you will get a good harvest."

"You can't plant no seed in a man, you plant an apple seed, and you end up with a watermelon. These men are not ready for no real relationships," Mini replied.

"Let me tell you all how to fertilize your seed so that you can get the best crop of men you can get. I have the master keys to unlock any type of relationship. I called them the ten fruits. Do you all want to hear about them?"

"Yeah, we do!" They all chimed in.

"Well, get your pens and paper," I said, swiping my thumb across my nose. "Class is in session!"

They all rushed to their stations and got paper, appointment books, or whatever they could find, and their pens. They drained their last sips of coffee, scarfed down their donuts, and gathered around to hear what The Great One had to say about men and relationships.

"Alright, girl scouts, here is what I want you to know and understand—it is possible to be a winner in relationships."

As I walked around and pushed each hooded dryer in the up position, I said, "I am not talking spiritually, who's right or who's wrong. I am not talking about the five rules that he is not into you. I'm not talking about that junk. Or if he does not open the car door, he is not the one. I'm showing you how to win in any given situation! You might ask who is accountable here? Who is responsible in this situation? Or you might say this is too hard to get over, but I promise you if you follow the steps that I am going to give you: YOU WILL WIN! This is real talk, not Hollywood, not the Real Housewives of Blah, Blah, Blah, but real men and real women issues and how to resolve them."

The ladies cried out, talking over each other, "We got a bunch of questions."

"I have a question about finances," Boonie said.

Mini sat up and pointed her pen at me. "I need to talk about 50/50 in a relationship."

"There are some sex questions I feel like I need to know," Camelot said.

"I need to know what is wrong with men. Why am I not getting this?" Guru shouted.

Putting my palms up in a stop position, I said, "Ok, ladies, one at a time."

CHAPTER 1

—— ✣ ——

Hidden Secrets

The keys to unlock what is already in you.

"THE FIRST AND the most important fruit—make sure you put this one in your memory bank—is Hidden Secrets. Hidden Secrets… you might ask what that means? Aren't secrets already hidden? Sometimes there really is not a secret at all but a piece to a puzzle, that when revealed, makes total sense, and you think it cannot be that easy. Oh, but it is that easy for a woman to get the full potential out of her relationships.

"All you need is a feather instead of an arm wrestle. Comforting, sweetness, and a soothing feminine spirit are the Hidden Secret. It is hidden in plain sight because it is an innate part of being a woman. It is like a loaded gun, and it is powerful.

"A woman has to be aware of her emotions. A woman needs to learn how to not misplace her emotions, and that has to be a significant part of her life."

"Please, Ramon, it ain't that easy," Mini said, giving Guru a high-five.

Sunshine sat up from a slouched position and put her pad on her lap, and said, "Yeah, I believe it really is that easy."

"What makes you say it is that easy? If it was that easy, we would all be happily ever after with some man somewhere. It is not always easy to be sweet and comforting when somebody is mean and hateful and making your life a living hell!" Mini expressed in a stern tone as her emotions flared up.

Now was my chance to catch their undivided attention. "You can put in your mind what you want a man to do. You have a gift that God has given you. You are a natural nurturer, you have great adaptability skills, you can adjust to any given situation, but that's not a man's natural ability. You can make him exercise that component. If you can conform to him and submit, then you have the power. You can make him conform to any way you want him to be. The greatest servant is the greatest leader. Be a great navigator.

"The following concepts are very important parts of your Hidden Secrets. You ladies really need to write these down:"

- *Submission* is power. It allows a man to let his guard down. When he lets his guard down, that tells him you believe and trust him. That is very fortifying to his psyche. Submission makes a man vulnerable. It is like kryptonite—it takes the fight out of him. He is powerless against your persuasion.

- *Motivating ability* is the fuel that can make a man go that extra mile. A man will stretch himself beyond measure, break barriers and go beyond limitations. The greatest motivation for a man is a woman.

- *Nurturing* is a natural ability of a woman. A woman knows how to feed a man whatever his needs are, whether he is hungry, tired, stressed. She knows how to fulfill those needs.

- *Intelligence* in a woman can make her the mind of reason in any situation. A woman has the quickness of wit, insight, and exceptional judgement. She makes nothing into something. She can take minor details in a man and turn it into something brilliant. Behind every great man is a great woman.

- *Comfort,* when used by a woman toward a man, is like serotonin. It changes his mood. Anything that is comfortable to a man is where he wants to be. The comforting arms of a woman is where a man will reveal his innermost secrets.

- *Faith* is the key to a woman's success when it comes to a man. When she believes in something, she becomes unshakeable. When a woman has that type of power and puts it behind a man, it could move a mountain. That type of energy can change anything.

- *Protective* is a quality that makes a woman want to safeguard and support her man no matter what. She becomes his extra eyes, his extra ears, and she knows how to protect him emotionally better than anyone.

"Listen up, kumquats, if you use these Hidden Secrets properly, you will never be disappointed. If you use them improperly, they can become disastrous. These secrets are innately in you already!"

Mini scrunched up her face in distaste. "I don't have to bow down to no man. Why should I have to submit to get along with him? I'm a strong, independent woman. My dad taught me to be tough! Yeah, a man has to treat me like my father because he gave me the best of everything—whatever I needed from him. He was Johnny on the spot, and he told me, "Don't settle for less."

Guru quickly interrupted. "Hold it! That's your dad, not your man. That's what you require, not your potential husband. His values may be different, so you have to look at him as your better half and not a father. Do you want your husband to treat you like his daughter? You know a man treats his wife differently than his daughter."

Sunshine shook her head and grabbed the nape of her neck. "Ladies, can I say a couple of things here based on my husband and daughter's relationship? My daughter sees what she wants in a man in how her father treats me; how we interact with one another. She also learns how to be good for a man by listening to her father tell her how to treat a man. For example, he will instruct her to learn how to cook, clean, and be a comforting virtuous woman. He tells her how to listen to her potential husband and not be a loud, cursing, and argumentative woman."

Sweet Pea threw her arms up in the air. "Man, that sounds like a male chauvinist and old-fashion. He is really teaching her to be so submissive. Yuck!! I want a man that treats me even better than my father. I want a man that does not expect me to be cooking and cleaning all day, and I need to be able to express how I feel without him saying I am argumentative."

Boonie said, "Wait a minute, I don't think Sunshine is saying be a doormat. She is trying to say, use what's already in you to get what you want. It's not what you do—it's how you do it. You can't operate a machine properly if you don't understand the functions. You need to learn them, so you can press the right buttons and know exactly what you are going to get for the right reasons. I know my man is eating the right fruits, and I am getting the right results."

Camelot shouted in amazement, "If a woman got all these hidden fruits, I'm going to plant some seeds and harvest some women. I don't need no man," she said, clapping her hands, shaking her head. "Give me a woman!"

We all had to laugh at that one as it continued to rain cats and dogs outside.

I did not mind the intimate conversation with the ladies, but I felt I really needed to set them straight on a few things.

"You all need to tap into your femininity, and it should come naturally for you. It should be instinctual to you as a woman. If it is difficult for you, or it does not come easy to implement these Hidden Secrets, then you need to reevaluate your 'stroft' side."

Sweet Pea, laughing, said, "Ramon, what the heck is 'stroft'?"

I replied, "Stroft is strong and soft put together. Being soft is strong. Focus on your gentler side. I want you all to know this is not about how to break up with someone or get a divorce. This is about taking the worst scenario and making it work for you. This leads to the second fruit, which is the difference between planting good seeds and planting bad seeds."

CHAPTER 2

Planting Seed

Whatever you plant is what you will get.
If you plant a negative seed, you will get negative
results. If you plant positive seeds, you will get
positive results.

"NO MATTER HOW bad your situation is, if you plant good seeds, you can turn it around. You can take a mess and make it marvelous. Listen up, ladies, when planting your seeds, you have to be self-aware. If you are not self-aware, you will never get into the soul of a man. You will never penetrate his surface. I am about to give you all a scenario."

Boonie passed around some grapes, and all eyes turned towards me. I took a few grapes and threw them in my mouth. They were sweet going down my throat.

"There was a young lady who had a new relationship with a gentleman. They were dating for a few months. One particular night they went out, and he saw a few female friends and spoke to them. Everything was cool, but about a week later, he came over to her house, and she said, "Here, I want to give you this bag." He looked at the bag and said, "What is this?" He thought to himself, *she has given me a gift; that is really cool!* When he looked into the bag, it was condoms. And she looked directly at him and told him, "If you're going to be out there, you need to use these because I do not want you to bring me back anything."

The guy was really into her, but he was thinking to himself, *She does not even trust me. Since she does not trust me, I might as well go out and do whatever.* She made him feel like what's the point of being good.

"I say this to say, if you sow good seeds, you will get a good crop. If you sow bad seeds, you will come up empty. Remember, women, you need to set the pace. You are the navigator and the mind regulator."

"I always expect the worst and hope for the best," Sweet Pea abruptly remarked.

"Why do you think that way?"

"Because I do not want to be disappointed. I do not want to get my hopes up high."

"It shows me the fear in your beliefs, and that gives birth to your behavior."

Sweet Pea swiftly cut me off, slightly jerking her neck, and she badgered the conversation. "I am not afraid of no man, but these men need to start acting their age. Why would you be smiling at other women and you out with your lady? I don't care if you knew them or not! If that is the case, why did he not introduce her to them?"

Jokingly I said, "Don't be jerking your neck at me," as Sweet Pea rolled her eyes.

Camelot laughed and instigated, "My male friend always be jerking his neck when he talks, and I don't like it either! He does it when he is getting smart with me, and I have to put him in check!"

I continued. "The seed starts in your heart, Sweet Pea. If you allow insecurities to control your thought process, then everything he does is going to be wrong. Everybody's intentions are not to hurt you! Those negative seeds can take over and control you and the person you care for.

"For instance, when I go out, I know a lot of women. I am not about to introduce my lady to everyone because they are acquaintances and are not a part of my inner circle. I do not want everyone in my business, so if they are not that important, I will not waste my time introducing them to my lady."

"Of course, you, like most men, know a lot of women and we women are expected to go with the flow," Mini said, adjusting her blouse. "You talk about planting seeds, but that is part of the problem with men—you all are planting too many seeds in too many places."

Guru said, "I'm not like that. If that had happened to me, I would not have waited until later. I am going to address it right then and there."

Boonie chimed in, "Yeah, my man was a manager at this company, and women would be calling him to go to lunch and out for drinks after work. One called too late, and man, I told her, 'do not let me have to come up there and beat the brakes off you!' See, I will go there."

"Alright, sheep, I know women have the herd mentality, where one follows the leader and falls off the cliff. I am trying to steer you away from the cliff. I am trying to teach you how to win!"

I needed a breeze because it felt like I was exerting a lot of energy, so I turned my face upward toward the ceiling fan. "You ladies are planting a seed, but you are not watering it, and it is going to shrivel up and die. You plant seeds in fear and not faith. When you plant a seed and do not water it, that's fear. You have to water it in faith. There are two ways women operate—fear or faith. Which one do you want to operate in? When you operate in faith, those are things you cannot see, but you make it happen."

The thunder pounded outside, and the lights flickered briefly. "A man wants a woman who can be his homie, lover, and friend. That sounds like a cliché, but it is the truth. He wants to be able to go out with you and feel free and be himself. He wants to actually believe you have faith in him."

Mini opened her mouth to say something, and I put my finger up to my mouth as a motion to be quiet and let me finish. "If you keep planting good seeds, you will see a change in his attitude, his work ethic, even his respect for you. There is so much power in planting positive seeds, but it starts in your heart. If you think wrong about a man, you will never treat him right, and whenever you have conflicts, he will always be wrong."

I thought to myself, *based on some people's facial expressions, these ladies were stirring up like a barn fire!* "For practical reasons, ladies, I'm going to tell you two scenarios. I am going to ask you to decide which scenario is a good seed and which one is bad. We want to make sure we all really understand.

"This is my first scenario. Are you listening, my little lilies?" I bent down and folded my arms on the back of my chair. "A close friend called me one day, and she was extremely upset with her man. For the last seven years, he had been in jail, and she had been visiting him, putting money on his book, and taking care of all his outside affairs. Right before he was about to be paroled, they started arguing really bad. The closer it came to him getting out, her insecurities started rearing their ugly head. When she would call me, she would be ranting and raving about how she had warned him that he needed to stay close to home and not be out here with all these women that carry diseases."

She would say, "He is not used to being out, and he doesn't know how these women are because he has been locked up for a while." They continued to have one petty argument after another. Due to their numerous disagreements, he decided he would not parole with her, but he would parole somewhere else.

"What do you ladies think about this scenario? Was it good seed or bad seed?"

Mini eyes got wide as golf balls, "This is what I am talking about! No good shiftless men! That's why I would never go with a jailbird! I have never been that frantic about a man! Clearly, she doesn't love herself, and you got to love yourself! No man will ever define me."

Sunshine rolled her eyes, "You are so cynical, Mini, when it comes to men! You said one bad thing after another about this man. Just because he went to jail does not make him a bad person. We all make mistakes. As far as this scenario, that was a bad seed because old girl was planting bad seeds in her relationship even before her man got out of jail."

Lightning struck, and we all flinched and looked out the window as the clouds unleashed a rigorous amount of rain as it pattered the roof.

Camelot swiveled around in her chair with a facetious smile on her face. "Yeah, she was worried about somebody getting that penis! I would say that is negative because I would not have been worried about that at all!"

"Camelot, don't be gross!" I replied.

"Ain't this about seed planting?"

Everyone started to laugh.

"I believe she saw herself with him in jail, but it was hard for her to imagine herself with him out. She could control him in jail because he was like a puppy in a cage, but the closer it came to him getting out, she started to be afraid that she would not be important to him," Guru stated.

"Eureka! Y'all some brain surgeons!" I said, clapping my hands together. "I think y'all got it!" I walked to Guru's chair and placed my hand on her shoulder. "Let me piggyback on what Guru said. This is what I believe. She allowed her fears to overtake her faith. Women love to have jail relationships with men because it is a fantasy, and fantasies feel good. Not only jailhouse romances, but dating sites and long-distance relationships are something women look forward to because it builds a comfort-level of control. I have been in many long-distance relationships."

They anxiously raised their hands to speak.

"Now wait a minute, just hear me out! Women get an invented vision stuck in their minds because it is a beautiful place. The quickest way to get into a woman's emotion is through her imagination. That's why if you write her a love letter, she can envision a fairy-tale that intrigues her. Women, unlike men, are not visual, they are emotional, and you can get to their emotions through words. That's why many women love romance novels because it gets in their imagination and translates to their emotions. You can make a fantasy be whatever you want it to be, but reality is disappointment, hurt, and pain, and that is real. If you want to woo a woman, just have a long-distance relationship, date site, or jailhouse relationship with them because that's a fantasy—it doesn't hurt. You don't have to deal with the real person. Trust me," I said as I winked one eye. "I know. Take it from the Great One."

Sunshine raised her eyebrows and tilted her head to one side. "This is so ironic, and you make a good point about the love letters. I was watching a historical program about Catherine of Argonne. Catherine of Argonne was married to

King Henry VIII, but she was promised to his older brother Arthur first. She came to meet Arthur for the first time before their marriage ceremony and was asking him about the love letter he wrote to her about wanting to kiss her on the neck and make love to her." Sunshine took a deep breath to slow herself down. "He did not know what she was talking about. Later on, she was talking to his younger brother, Henry, and she could tell by the way he was talking to her and how the ladies seemed to like him—that he was the one who'd written the love letters. Arthur confronted Henry and asked him why he wrote those letters because he could tell that his future wife was in love with his brother and not him. Henry told Arthur, 'I wrote the letters trying to help you out because you are not good with words.' She married Arthur because she was promised to him, but he died soon after their marriage. She ended up marrying his brother, King Henry VIII."

I said, "Look at old Henry. He was like the candy bar sweet! They were mackin' back in the 1500s! Ladies, do you got anything to say?"

Mini crossed her legs and sat back in her chair, and said, "Wow."

Boonie looked around at each lady. "I'm not sure if I am the only one that is not understanding what writing love letters and jailhouse romances have to do with planting seeds?" she said, turning toward her mirror and spraying her hair with some oil sheen.

That was her special hairspray that lingered in my nose and always seemed to burn my nostrils when she spayed it. I fanned my hand. "Listen up, Einstein! If you don't understand what's broken, how can you fix it? You may have to go beyond the surface, dig down in layers. That is why people have these types of relationships, so they will not feel threatened. That is the only way they can stay in control. Insecurities always lead people to plant bad seeds in a relationship."

I wiped off my station that had gotten greasy with hairspray and walked to the coffee pot to relieve my nostrils, and threw out the empty donut box. "Alright, here's the second scenario. Put on your thinking caps!

"One of my clients came into the salon, and she was not her usual talkative self. I swiveled the chair around and asked her, 'Are you ok?' Her eyes welled up with tears, and she shook her head no.

"Just tell me what is the matter."

She sighed heavily. "A couple of days ago, this woman called my phone and told me she had been sleeping with my husband for three years, and he had just left her house. By the way, she mentioned, 'I have been over your house in your bed on more than one occasion.'

"I reached over to my station and grabbed some tissue as she sniffled.

"Anyway, when he got home, I confronted him because I knew she had to get my number out of his phone. I told him, 'You know your girlfriend for the last three years just called me.'

He said, 'That woman is just trying to break up my marriage, and she is mad because I refuse to leave you. She is an ex-girlfriend that has been trying to get me back for the longest time. Because I was not trying to get back with her, then threats came. I told her to do what you have to do.'

'I asked him, had she been in our bed?'

'Naw, I did not have her in our bed, she lyin! She will say anything to break us up.'

'Well, she did break us up,' I said as I took my ring off and threw it at him. I screamed, 'Get Out Now!'

'I'm about to get a divorce, and I never thought it would come to this! He has been away for a week, and I miss my best friend,' she sobbed.

"I said, 'Listen, are you still in love with him?'

'Yes, I miss him, and my heart is broken!'

'Has he been calling you?'

'I have not been answering the phone, and he leaves messages about how sorry he is, he loves me, and doesn't want to lose me.'

'Here is the situation; you could be heartbroken, and you could lose him. That's a lot of hurt. Now I am going to ask you something, do you want to be bitter and heartbroken, or do you want to be healed?

She said, 'I want to be healed.'

"If you want him back, understand this. I would not leave a man that I'm in love with. Because it is very difficult to be away from someone you love, at least he's there. Let me show you how to win at this point. I would take him back and tell him that I forgive him, and you know he is a good man and that he regrets what he did. Tell him, 'I know you love me, that you are really not like that, and I forgive you wholeheartedly.'

He is in your debt, whatever you want or anything you cannot afford, he will get for you right now."

'Well, I did want a new refrigerator, a new stove, and my kitchen decorated. I want a new bedroom set, and I want to trade in my car.'

"This is going to make forgiveness go down a lot easier. If he loves you, he will give you all the things you ask him for. He is going to invest in you and where your interest is, is where your heart goes. Your relationship will build back up, but remember this, when you forgive him, when you get those gifts, never bring it back up. I promise you this, you will start working on building your relationship and always have faith in him. You have to act like you believe and trust him.

"She later told me she forgave him and got all the things that she asked for—her refrigerator, stove, car, everything.

"She thanked me and said, 'Things are awesome! Our relationship is great!'

"Think about it like this: one man 20 chances or 20 men with one chance?

"Tell me, what seed is this?"

"Oh Oh Oh, I know, I know," Guru shouted as she secured the bag, "that's a good seed!"

Boonie said, "I would forgive him with some stitches, but it's the good one!'"

Mini said, "I would not let that bum off the hook for nothing! He could buy all those things, and I would leave him. And if I stayed, I would make his life a living hell!"

"Now that is a bad seed!"

Everyone was rocking in their seats, cracking up!

"Bad seeds lead to Spoiled Fruit…"

CHAPTER 3

— ❧ —

Spoiled Fruit

Selfish to a point that you become rotten.

BOONIE QUICKLY ASKED, "What do you mean by Spoiled Fruit?"

"Boonie, I hear your question, and I plan to explain in detail what Spoiled Fruit is, but first, I want to address Mini. Mini, I sympathize with you, but let me get one thing straight. No one wants to be cheated on. It hurts and it's painful. You can't stop a person's behavior, but you can curb it to some degree. If you truly love that person and plan on staying with them, you must forgive them and reap the benefits. This is how you win! Don't focus on cheating because no one is perfect."

Mini became irate. "I had six uncles, my grandfather, and my father, and they all cheated on their wives, and their wives did not leave them. They more than likely were good women. I asked my uncles, 'Why do you all cheat?' They said this is what men do!"

Mini's turbulent emotions led me to use a sympathetic tone. "When infidelities happen, it may momentarily derail you, but it is not over for you. There is always a light at the end of the tunnel."

Sweet Pea responded, "I have been on both sides. I have been married, the side piece, and I have been in several committed relationships. I am so tired of men thinking they can do whatever they want to do, and us women are supposed to accept it."

"Listen, come on now! If you want to learn, you can't have tunnel vision. It is going to be hard for you to understand me. Open your mind and be diplomatic. This is a new way of thinking. If you go back to your old behavior with the same mind, you are going to get the same results.

"Now I know, some men have a lust problem, but that can be tamed. Don't focus on cheating, focus on forgiveness. That's not only good for you but good for the relationship, and that is what will bring him closer to you. He knows you are better than him because you have a gentle and tender heart. See, that's what we fall in love with."

I walked toward the center of the floor and directed my attention to all the ladies. "Men are different from women. They are wired differently. One reason you like men is that they are different from you. Let's define what the perfect man is; he is always a gentleman, opens doors, he is polite and complimentary, he makes lots of money which he spends all on you. That's good, right? The perfect man. You think that's what you want, but I can tell you that is not what you really want at all. That kind of man will never make you happy. An ideal man is a man that is flawed. He is not better than you, and he needs you to complete him. A woman is a natural nurturer and fixer. She instinctively knows how to do those things. She can look at your outfit, your house, and your life and know how to fix them all to make them better. She needs a man that needs her (not a train wreck) but a normal guy with flaws (color blind, a bit of a slob, not good with numbers, etc.)."

Sweet Pea touched her temples as if this conversation was wreaking her nerves. "This is too much to keep a man. I'm not willing to go through all that!"

"What? Too much!!" I shook my head and turned toward Sweet Pea. "I bet you are probably using your Hidden Secrets everywhere but where they should be used. You speak life into everything except your relationship. You nurture everybody except your man. You help everybody out with their problems, but when it comes to your man, he is the problem. You go to work and honor your boss, but don't give your man any respect. You nurture your kids, but you don't know how to nurture your man at all. You have faith in everything you do and everybody, but no faith in your man. You use your Hidden Secrets all over the place, but you don't use them in the most important place of all, which is your relationship. You will make up a holiday to nurture your girlfriend, but you won't make up with your guy to nurture him!"

I walked to the window and looked out. My thoughts were, *"Man, that water is getting high. I guess it's meant for us to be having this lesson."* I turned around and focused back on my girls.

"I am telling you these gems because I love you, and I want you to win in your relationships."

Camelot jumped up, singing, "Whatta Man, Whatta Man, Whatta Mighty Good Man!" as she gyrated.

Everybody said, "Girl, keep your day job and sit down!"

"What is the holiday for girlfriends? I'm interested in that!" Camelot asked.

"You haven't heard about it? I'm surprised you haven't heard about it! It's called Galentine's Day!" It's like Valentine's Day but for your girlfriends."

Everybody laughed about it.

"Settled down, ladies. I'm going to explain Spoiled Fruit through a series of anecdotes. Check this out!"

"A dude said, 'Baby, I am going downtown for a minute.' He came back three or four hours later.

'Where were you?'

'Downtown!'

'It doesn't take you 3 or 4 hours to go downtown. You were out with someone.'

"Next time, he is going to tell her a lie. She is an accuser, and this is what spoils relationships right here!"

"What is wrong with her asking where he is going?" Camelot asked.

"Buckwheat, please!!"

"Ramon is always calling somebody names! He is verbally abusive!'

I hit my hand, and said "Bam! Zoom!" and pointed my finger to the sky.

"Shut up and listen!"

Camelot grabbed her pen and pad and looked up and made a stink face, and licked her tongue out at me.

"Here is another anecdote for ya. A man gets up in the morning and asks where his coffee is, and you say, 'right here.' Or he asks if his lunch is ready, and you say, 'Yes.' That man goes to work and can work 12 hours straight and feel like he can conquer the world. You will be in his thoughts all day. That is the opposite of Spoiled Fruit."

Sunshine eased her comment in nice and slow. "There is nothing wrong with making your husband coffee and lunch even if he did not work 12 hours because that is something you should do."

"Good Job! The next story is not really an anecdote but something that actually happened to me for real. This will really drive home Spoiled Fruit.

"This was my own long-distance fantasy relationship, where it lasted for a year and a half before we moved in with each other. We talked on the phone and saw each other twice a month on the weekends. We decided to get married. We made the decision for me to uproot and move where she was. That was cool. We got a chance to interact with each other on a daily basis. There were some things about her that were quite different. She had an evil twin inside of her. One day, she showed me a collection of her videos. They were great videos, but to my surprise, my girl was 100 pounds heavier in the videos. My girl, for whatever reason, thought she was unattractive and that no one really wanted her, which was completely untrue. My point is, sometimes we think we need to change our outer appearance, but we really need to change our inner being so much more.

"One day, she and her girlfriend were in the car listening to R&B music, and instead of rocking with them, my thoughts were *put this gospel CD in, she will love it!* After we got home, her girlfriend put a bug in her ear. 'Girl, why you let him dictate what we gonna listen to?! I would go in there and curse him out and let him know, don't you never disrespect me like that!' She came in after I went to bed and woke me up with the foulest language. This chick had crossed the line, so I was leaving in the morning. Then she begged me to stay, "Please,

please, please." I agreed to stay with one stipulation—that we could not have any more episodes like this one for the next thirty days. We lasted for thirty days, but then she tapped the phone so that she could hear all the calls. She became violently angry if I was a little late getting home. It seemed like her whole existence was based on catching me doing something wrong. Finally, the decision was made for me to go back home but not before she changed the locks and refused to give me all of my possessions."

"That hoe was crazy!" Guru said.

"That's the kind of crazy that will make you turn straight!" Camelot said, putting her pencil down, stood and puckered her lips to put on her cherry red lipstick, primping in the mirror.

"That was the poster child of Spoiled Fruit, and this is why. They are so used to things going wrong, they seek out negative energy to vibe on it. Because they are more familiar with disappointment. They become comfortable with being the victim. In every relationship, they find a way to become the damsel in distress. Even if the guy is not making them the victim, they will cut a backdoor out to make a way for them to be the victim. Some people like making a problem where there is none and will react better in a relationship that is full of issues that they can fix. If there is nothing to fix, they are miserable and will start arguments and keep up strife just so they can have something to destroy.

"So, when you ladies listen to your girlfriends, this is something maybe you shouldn't do. People see that weakness in you and know you are a magnet for negative energy, and they give you what you want for their benefit."

Sunshine got up and walked to the water dispenser and got a cup of water, and came back to her seat. "Sometimes we do listen to our friends, we have to stop that. They will tell us one thing and do something else, and not only that, how can a woman tell us about a man because she is not a man? She doesn't know how a man feels. If you want some advice about women, you ask a woman, and if you want advice about a man, ask a man."

"What do you all get from this?"

"I got from this: Most women have rotten fruit that makes toxic relationships which add up to judging the relationship out of fear," Sunshine explained.

I slammed my fist on the back of my chair. "You can't, dog-gone it, allow your girlfriend's insecurities to resonate with yours.

That's when the rotten begins within you. Be mindful of who you listen to. You cannot remove rot from fruit once it has gone bad. But the good news is, it is never too late to find good fruit. You rationalize your friend has your back with easy negative solutions. Easy negative solutions come at a cost to your relationships.

"Don't be a slave to your emotions. Instead of talking too much, you should probably pay attention, ya dig! Listen to your man. He will tell you how to get what you want because your girlfriend can't."

Sweet Pea placed her hands on the arms of the chair and pushed up and stood, eager to speak. "Who else am I supposed to talk to? My girls are always there for me when men come and go!"

"Your friends are commendable for being there for you, they have your best interest at heart, but bad communications spoil good habits. There is a difference between understanding and understood. They look alike, but they are not the same. Understanding means you comprehend what I say. Understood means you execute it.

"How many bad relationships have you all had? Put the number up with your fingers. Ok, 20 or 30."

"Stop playin," they all shouted.

"I'm kiddin. 2, 3, 9; Ok, that's good. Let me ask you all a question. In the relationship, whose fault was it that you broke up?"

There was an echo in unison, "Theirs!!!"

"Something told me y'all were going to say that.

"It is not possible in all these relationships that it was completely the other person's fault. Here's the problem: you all never learned anything. You stayed at that level and did not grow, and you never learned from your mistakes. So, when you had more relationships, and it did not work, you became more bitter. Your expectations became more difficult to obtain. Men are hunters. They don't have to like but one thing about you. They will give you what you want to get what they want. They will take you out to the show and to dinner, all that, and be done with you. They already know you are not on their level, and you continually watch them to perfect their mistakes instead of growing from your mistakes. You are looking for the person to have grown, and you stood still, that leads to a devious mind."

CHAPTER 4

Devious Minds

*Devious Minds will lead to the dismantling of a
relationship unknowingly.*

MINI EXPLODED, "MEN don't want nothing but sex. That's all
they want!"

"Is that what you got from that? That is not what he was
saying," Sunshine added.

Camelot stood up and spread her arms. "You sound just
like them ladies—still on that first-grade level!"

Sunshine slightly tapped herself on the forehead and
looked in Mini's direction. "This is what he is saying, you cannot expect them to grow, and you do not. Then you start having all these insinuations saying, 'if you were a real man, you
would be doing this,' he should be calling, or if he was a real

man, he would allow me to express myself. My girlfriends are always talking about what the other person did but never realizing what they have done. Just because they were wrong does not mean you were right."

Sweet Pea's voice raised several octaves, causing her mouth to widen and spittle shot from her lips in several directions. "What you just said, that was cool, but I have an issue with a man that has a problem with me expressing myself. No man should feel less than a man if a woman wants to talk about the problems in the relationship. He is not mature or even on my level if he feels he cannot rise to my expectations. I'm not a first-grader, so don't treat me like one!"

I walked to the door and looked out, everybody was getting very excited. Even the rain seemed to get excited, it was bouncing off the ground like jumping beans.

"It's very good to be expressive. The problem is not expression," I said, walking back to my seat and sat down. "Expression is a beautiful thing, but what are you expressing? If your mind is in a good place and it is creating a nurturing atmosphere, then you know your expression is correct." The vibe in the salon had changed, and it was calm once again. "If you get the opposite effect, then you need to know that something must be wrong. Expression is supposed to draw attention, not run it away."

"Here are some bullet points to let you know if you have a devious mind. Write these down:"

- Private Investigator - invading a person's privacy - checking cell phone, stalking social media
- Accuser - you are always looking for a problem, be it cheating or lying
- Tit for Tat - looking to retaliate at every turn
- Controlling - they have to be in charge of everything
- Con Artist - always trying to get something for nothing
- Narrow Minded - can only envision things your way
- Hypocritical - constantly putting up a pretense and passing judgement

Everything got quiet as you could see them concentrating on their notes. Slowly, my eyes gazed around the salon and did a survey.

Boonie was patting her feet on the floor, leaning forward as if she was writing deep diary secrets.

Camelot had her leg on the rim of her chair, with a mischievous grin, as she steadily stroked her pen on the pad, probably in case she decided to explore those options to switch hit.

Sunshine glanced over at Sweet Pea with a soothing smile and started compiling her notes.

Sweet Pea sat there soaking up what was said while she regained her composure. Contemplating the discussion, she tapped her pen with reservation.

Guru seemed to be getting a heightened clarity of what was being revealed as she moved her pen across the paper.

Mini sat straight up with perfect posture, and moved her arm and intentionally hesitated to write. She appeared to be having a tug of war with the pen on what bullet points to focus on.

As I looked at the girls, I thought to myself, *they have so much internal beauty in them, and if I can get them to see and understand how to use it, they would never lose. I really hope they don't think that I'm doing this to be critical, but sometimes constructive criticism is necessary. Even though they might feel I'm saying something that may hurt their feelings. It is vital they understand what I'm saying and make it work for them. I want to equip them to be champions when it comes to challenges. Life is going to have some bumps and bruises, everything may not go smoothly, but the correct mindset could propel them into that place where they need to be. You want them to be soft as a lamb but have the strength of a lion.*

I took my comb and hit my station like a gavel. "Hey ladies! How many of you'll have gone through a man's phone, checked his social media, or stalked a man?"

"Who hasn't gone through a man's phone before?" Sweet Pea asked arrogantly. "I don't normally go through a man's phone, but I did, and he had all kinds of photos of naked women. I'm tired of all these no-good men lying and pretending to be something that they are not. He acted like he was this church going dude. I'm thinking to myself, let me check his phone to see if he got women's numbers or photos. Who wants to be dealing with a phony man?"

Sunshine looked up in surprise. "Sweet Pea, you know that sounds real insecure, personally snooping through somebody's phone is unhealthy whether you find something or not. But what you need to do is get to the root of your distrust and address that! If you are at the point in your relationship that you are willing to break his trust in you by invading his privacy, something in you is broken. You are worse than him. How would you like a man to be going through your purse? That's a lot of game playing to me," she said as she swatted her hand. "What does naked women in his phone have to do with how he treats me? As long as he treats me well, I don't have time to be a private investigator!"

Clearing my throat, I said, "Sweet Pea, that is game playing, and that signals bad intentions. The minute you go through a man's phone, car, e-mail, pockets, wallet, or any of his personal stuff, that shows irrational fear in the relationship. You are the one not honest. If you get more peace out of snooping than trusting, then you need to examine what your problem is." Even though tough love was necessary, I elaborated.

"As far as the naked photos, he probably had them before he got with you and never took them out. Regardless of that, how you think about him is what will break you up before those photos will. If you think wrong about him, you will never treat him right. Once you think wrong about someone, the relationship is doomed. Anytime you do something like that, you are no earthly good—that is a Devious Mind."

I stepped around my chair, eased over to Sweet Pea, and bent down, and gave her a hug to keep her from talking over me, and whispered, "You do not always have to have the last word, ok?" She looked at me with the evil eye.

"Many times, private investigation will lead you to be an accuser. Who among you accused someone of cheating?"

Mini jumped up all bright-eyed and bushy-tailed. "Here is a story of an accuser that happened to me personally! One night while sleeping, the Lord woke me up, told me my significant other was cheating on me, and to get in my car and drive to some hotels. Man, I went across town and looked in every hotel parking lot. On my way home, there was a little motel to the left of me and in the parking lot was his car with his license plate. The only thing on my mind was to confront him. The next day when he came over, we got into it real bad! He lied and said he was at the hotel at a card party."

Guru cracked up. "Girl, you are a fool! A card party? Well, did you believe that?"

"Hell to the Naw! I tried to knock his head off. He acted like he was going to hit me, and then I went and got my gun and said, 'you are a lying sum sum. You were in that motel with another woman!"

Boonie asked, "What happened? Did y'all stay together?"

"We did not break up right away, but the trust was gone. Eventually, he just faded away because he knew he could not get away with nothing. My womanly intuition and discernment were always going to let me know when he was up to something."

Sunshine was rocking back and forth in her chair as her neck jerked with hysterical laughter.

Sweet Pea clapped her hands. "Won't he do it! I'm that same way, girl! That happened to me too in a way. Me and this dude really connected for about 6 months. We talked on the phone for hours. He would come over and watch movies. Then, all of sudden, he stopped calling. Every time we talked, he would abruptly get off the phone and not call me back. He stopped coming over to my place. When he finally came over, I decided to confront him because my spiritual discernment told me he was secretly married. 'Why don't you call me back? Why don't you ever invite me to your place? Are you married?' He told me, 'No,' but I knew he was lying because he stopped calling me after that. A month later, that dummy was in Red Lobster with some woman a few tables across from me. That probably was his wife."

Ramon Darnell

Camelot threw her hands in the air. Her body language spoke a thousand words.

"Are you all kidding me?" I asked with a chuckle. "I'm not super spiritual or nothing from my recollection; what y'all said doesn't have anything to do with the Lord, thank you. When you are talking about spirituality, that comes with faith, believing in something that you cannot see. Not being in some kind of confusion where it causes strife. When you have faith, whatever that situation is, it turns it around because you believe, not accusing someone. Satan is the author of confusion, not the Lord."

Guru dropped her pen, and I picked it up and handed it to her and said, "Things are going to go wrong sometimes, but how do you fix it? A man ain't perfect, so understand that. Like I told you before, when you go into a relationship, you must believe that he's good and he's kind, and even when you think he's done something wrong, you let him know that you believe in him 100%. If you do these things, he will give you his mind, body, and soul. That's a promise. Instead of giving him all types of ultimatums, that's stupid. Using unnecessary energy to tear him down, use that to build him up."

I strode back to my chair with my arms behind my back like a college professor. "You are steadily trying to catch a man. What are you trying to catch him for? What is your angle? You ain't going to get nothing but a heartache! I'm trying to show you how to win. I'm trying to show you how to get your man to worship you.

"I can't allow y'all to be around me and be goofballs! You're going to be great women! Y'all not going to be goofballs on my watch!"

My voice became passionate with emphasis. "Do not follow a man in the middle of the night to find out if he is cheating. Do not accuse a man of being married if he doesn't call you back within a certain time period. If you're not any good, don't blame it on the man, don't go out and do stuff and blame him. He can't make you do things against your principles if you need him to justify your wrongdoing; it's already in you. You got a dirty Devious Mind."

"A dirty devious mind? Ain't that a bit much?" Boonie inquired.

"If you are still confused about a dirty devious mind, let me give you an example. Let's say a couple is shopping for groceries. An attractive woman walks down the same aisle as them in the opposite direction. The woman looks at her man to see if his eyes are following the attractive woman. Instantly, she starts accusing him of having a wandering eye. The man emphatically tells his woman he was not looking at the other woman at all. She insists he was, and they argue about it. Now he does not want to go anywhere with her because he does not want to be a prisoner in the relationship. He doesn't want to feel as if he is on a leash like a dog.

"Big things take care of themselves, and it is the little things that become monumental. Because you have a devious mind, stop trying to make a man worse than you are. You are going to make him leave you. If you women want to get to another level or get a different type of man, then you need to have a divine mind, not a devious one. If you use the Hidden Secrets we discussed earlier, then if he looked at a million women, it would not make any difference because his mind would boomerang back to you every time.

"Now being an accuser many times rolls into Tit for Tat, which is my next bullet point."

Remarkably everyone was quite silent, so I continued. "Here is a perfect example of Tit for Tat: dude was 30 minutes late getting home, and he and his woman were going out. She got mad and put on her night-clothes and told him they were not going. Dude is chronically late, so you might have to assist him with his time management skills."

Mini asked, "Do you guarantee that he will give me the stars, the moon, and everything in between if I put my devious mind behind me and help him to be the best he can be? I'm only human and can only handle so much, especially if he is this egotistical butthole that is always late."

"This is not for him but for you, goofball. That is why I'm giving you examples. It's to make you a better person. What he does is not contingent on what you do."

Camelot said, "Yeah, women can be catty. That's one thing I know."

Sunshine stated, "I'm not a tit-for-tat person. If I like you, I'm not going to go tit-for-tat. If I have to do that, then that relationship is over."

I walked briskly over to Mini and said it with such passion that she gave me her undivided attention. "Listen! Little things can alter your relationship. For example, you feel that you can't trust him as far as you can see him. You're like a warden! Your insecurities have controlled your whole being because your stinking thinking has messed up your mind. You stay on something negative. Why can't it be on something good? When you care for someone, you should think loving thoughts; not if he is 30 minutes late, then no dinner, no sex, no comfort. The only thing you're getting is an argument. Crazy! All because you have the wrong thoughts in your head."

Sweet Pea raised her hand as if she was in school. "Can I ask you a question? You keep giving examples. Here is my example. What do you do if you text someone, call someone, and they do not text or call you back for days, and when they do, they want something from you? 9 times out 10, it is probably sex. How do you teach them a lesson and let them know you do not like how they are treating you? You have to teach them by not calling them back or telling them no when they want sex or a meal or help with something or other!"

I walked behind my chair. "Good question. You think whatever a man does to you, you're going to do it back. That's a devious mind because all you wanted was a reason to do what you wanted to do! You want to withhold something—you want to be retaliatory. That makes you no better than him. Just because he does it, you're going to do it too. If he jumped out the window, you would go jump out the window too. You are using that to justify what you want to do. You are trying to control him.

"Let me tell you this, it is better to use a feather than a hammer. In this scenario, if the dude has not called you back in several days, you need to figure out what made him not call in the first place. More than likely, you are more focused on yourself and not paying attention to him. I don't want to tell you this, but you are probably not giving him any reason to rush back to you! Let's give him a reason starting now. Find out the things he likes to do. What does he need? What comforts him? Are you talking too much, are you too controlling, are you giving him ultimatums? The only reason he will want to come by is for sex, and soon, that will not be enough. In a minute, he will not be calling at all because he will not want to be bothered with you. You are too busy focusing on what you want that you do not have a clue about what he likes."

"When you give into a man that's being weak. If he wants to get the best out of me, then he needs to know what I expect out of him!" Mini replied.

"Actually, you are weak when you react that way because when you make a sacrifice, that's being strong. It is easy to react to your emotions, but it is very hard not to be tit-for-tat. Constantly being tit-for-tat can lead to fast death or slow death to a man's ego. Control only lasts for so long—comfort lasts forever. Instead of using your controlling ways for evil, use your power of persuasion for good."

"What do you mean by our power of persuasion?" Guru asked.

"That question leads me to my next bullet point about being Controlling in a relationship.

"There is a difference between controlling and the power of persuasion. Controlling is always having to have it your way. You are constantly challenging a man's honor. Certain men cannot be controlled but can be easily persuaded."

Sunshine quickly jumped in and commented. "Some men are not easily persuaded, they do not trust women, they get what they want and dump them."

"The power of persuasion is already in you, in those Hidden Secrets that I revealed to you. It is lying dormant, and you do not know it is there. You are planting the wrong seeds when you think to yourself it is hard to persuade a man. You are already setting yourself up for failure.

"Check this out." I slapped my fist to the palm of my other hand. "We are going to go biblical for a minute. If you doubt anything I have been saying to you, let's look at history. If you want to know the power of a woman's ability to persuade, the bible has three instances. The first man was Adam, and God gave him a direct order not to eat the fruit. Eve beguiled him, and he did eat. The strongest man was Samson, and God told him not to share the secret of his strength. He was coerced by Delilah into revealing it. The wisest man was Solomon, and a woman convinced him to praise idol gods in the temple, and he knew God commanded him not to. Even though these women persuaded these Holy men to do evil, how much better it would have turned out if the women had used their power of persuasion for good?"

Camelot pulled her patented leather pants higher into her crotch and questioned softly, "So, it's the woman's fault that Adam ate the fruit, and we are evil?"

"No, I'm not saying that! The last thing God made was the strongest. It was a woman. God called her a good thing. If you use your power of persuasion wrong, it will corrupt your relationship, but the right way will manifest an incredible connection. That's why I'm trying to get you to see those Hidden Secrets."

"In the biblical days, really? Guru asked, "That's the women from back then; this is now!"

Sunshine explained. "Women are the same. We still use the same tools that are inbred in us. From generation to generation, it is the same principle."

I added to what Sunshine explained. "Let me explain something to y'all. Women have been controlling men from the beginning until now. Women back in the day did not even have the authority to set up laws or enforce the rules, but behind the scenes, they were making all the moves. They were making things happen. Man, y'all better get it together. If you cannot persuade a man to do what you want and need him to do, then y'all ain't no good! How many times do I need to tell you that? Stop blaming it on him since you are not using what you have."

My words were bursting like a volcano ready to erupt. "Stop trying to be a con artist! The only way to be conned is trying to get something for nothing. That brings me to my next bullet point...

"Ladies, have you ever gone along with a relationship and got what you wanted out of it without putting any work in?"

"Yeah, but what does that have to do with being conned?" Boonie asked.

"A woman accepting half of a man rather than having no man at all is the definition of a con artist, and the reason is it's being selfish when you settle for less to get the things you want. You gotta remember, you have to be better than a man without being the careless one in the relationship."

"Give me an example of what it is to be careless in a relationship since men are the careless ones." Mini put in her two cents as she pointed her finger toward me.

"You become careless when you focus more on what you are getting and not on him. Ladies, you'll get the things you want for a while, but you're going to get more than you bargained for if you take a lesser man."

Sunshine asked, "What do you mean by a lesser man? Do you mean the crackhead on the corner, an alcoholic, the jobless brother, the man still at home with his mother?"

"It does not have to be like that. He could be rich but be poor in character—a man with no morals. It's like trying to get something for nothing. You can't settle for less and expect the best. It's a natural instinct for a man to feel that a woman is better than him. When you become worse, that attracts a man worse than you. If you think in a selfish manner, you have a devious mind, then you drop a level when it comes to morals, and you're going to be a magnet to men of a lower level."

The atmosphere simmered down from a fiery flame to a small campfire roast. "Alright, girl scouts, this brings us to my next bullet point, which is Narrow-Minded." Everyone sat up in their chairs with expectations, pens ready to write.

"People who cannot take constructive criticism are narrow minded. Criticism has to be your best friend. It helps you to become better." My mind paused, wondering if I was being too scientific, sounding like a charm school teacher or some kind of drill sergeant, naaah… maybe not.

"Women will sometimes get into their feelings, and they only think about how they feel. When their partner tries to communicate to them their side of the story, they refuse to listen, and they only envision how they feel. Many times, you can identify with this by this particular behavior. If your significant other is talking to you and they only can get four words out of their mouth before you cut them off, then that is being narrow-minded. Basically, you are refusing to listen to them, and it is all about you. The trick about this is similar to what I said previously. Many times, if you take the time and be quiet and pay attention to the other person, they will tell you how to get what you want."

Sweet Pea stood up. "You keep telling us how to get what we want. Narrow-minded is what men are! A narrow-minded person is a person who does not listen to other's opinions, thoughts, or feelings and only sees things their way. That's what men do when they do not call or text you back so that you can communicate your feelings."

I gazed out the window. It was very ironic how it started to rain heavily outside. Was this a sign? The song suddenly came to mind, *Can You Stand the Rain* by New Edition.

"Sweet Pea, all throughout this conversation, you have never been wrong about anything. The reason why you have all of these problems is strictly because you don't use your Hidden Secrets. Be less eager to express yourself, and be more willing to listen. Let me tell you the difference between hearing and listening. Hearing, you have a choice but listening is the intent to obey."

I swung Sweet Pea toward the mirror, standing behind her. I could smell her perfume that reminded me of Jasmine as it wafted around the room.

"Look at you, you're beautiful, tall, fly and smell good, by the way! You have many great things about you, but they alone are not working for you. Try my way! Use what you already have hidden inside of you."

As Sweet Pea looked at herself, her eyes welled up with tears. Camelot handed her a tissue and gave her a big, long hug. Sweet Pea swatted her hands and said, "Get back, get back" Everyone started to laugh, and it took the tension out of the air.

"I'm going to try, Oh Great One," she smirked.

"My final bullet point is Hypocritical, and what that means is you are always passing judgment on what someone else is doing without examining yourself. Almost every statement, comment, or question you ladies have made throughout this discussion has been hypocritical. Does anyone want to address that?" You could hear crickets. Everyone was gazing in the mirror at themselves and each other.

"Ok, get out the mirrors. Here are a few scenarios when you say you don't curse and you have a disagreement with your boyfriend, and you start cursing, and he asks you, 'I thought you didn't curse?' You turn around and say, 'I don't normally curse, but you made me mad. You got under my skin.' That's a hypocrite. You say you don't drink, but on special occasions, you drink—that is hypocritical. Stop pretending to be something you're not. You say, 'I don't eat pork; it's against my religion,' and he tells you, 'we have so much in common, baby, I don't eat pork either.' One day you come home early and catch him eating pork chops, and now that you caught him, you say to yourself, "I'm going to make me a pork chop with gravy with onions on top.' When he comes home, you are going to be eating a big pork chop with gravy and onions on top, then he is going to say to you, 'I thought you didn't eat pork?' 'I don't eat pork. But when I saw you eating pork, it pissed me off, and now I'm eating it. It's all your fault, and you're to blame for me eating pork chops.'

"All I know is this story made me hungry!" Camelot said with her eyes closed and her nose flared as she inhaled a deep breath. "I can smell gravy and pork chops with onions now!"

"The point is this, can't nobody make you do something you don't want to do. It is something you wanted to do anyway.

They can introduce you to it, but they cannot make you do it. Women think they have everything on the ball and wonder why they can't get a better selection. It's because in your heart, you are a hypocrite. You have to become a better selection. If you want your selection of men to change, your heart has to change. So, when a woman talks about how dirty or bad her man is, she's only mirroring herself because a woman is the reflection of her man, no doubt. Y'all hypocrites."

"Not trying to beat anyone up, but let me say this—if you can identify the problem, then you can fix it. When you recognize a devious mind that can keep you from believing in false truths."

CHAPTER 5

False Truths

Believing your own lies are the truth; they will
falsely accuse you to believe their own truth.

"HERE ARE A few False Truths. Let me know what you think about each of them.

"He doesn't ever bring me flowers; he acts like he doesn't care about me—that's a false truth."

Sweet Pea sorted through her pad. "I have a lot of notes, and I'm getting there, but if he does not bring flowers or act romantic, how will I know he cares about me? Explain that."

"That's a false truth because some men have different customs. They may not be a flower and candy person, but that does not mean they do not care about you and let me tell you why. Men have various ways of expressing their love and affection. For instance, a man might display his love by simply wanting to watch the game with his favorite girl. It is better to understand someone than make someone do something. That is a better defense."

My walk was slow and intentional while I paced the floor back and forth. "Let me share something with y'all. My client told me about a situation with her boyfriend of 10 years. She said her man is not romantic at all. He does not give her flowers, no cards on Valentine's Day—no nothing ever. But yet he gives those kinds of gifts to his mother and daughter. She told him that it really bothers her. He said those things are not an expression of love. She asked him, 'If those things are not an expression of love, why do you give those types of gifts to your mom and daughter?' He said those were little gifts, so they will not think he had forgotten about them. So, for the past 3 months, she said he has not paid my car note, or my rent, or taken me out to dinner. When I asked him what was up, he told me to go look in the bedroom. There were three dozen roses, a card, and candy. He went on to say, 'That's what you wanted, and that's what you are going to get.' The question she asked me was, 'Why can't he value my feelings?'

"My answer to her was this: 'Women are never satisfied, and feelings are not always worth value. Just because you feel a certain way doesn't make it right. At some point, emotional maturity has to kick in. Sometimes, you have to put your feelings to the side and do a check and balance. Is it more important to give you flowers than take care of your needs? Pick your battles, every fight is not a battle, and every situation is not a battle to be won. Clearly, his expression of love was not flowers and candy. She took her eyes off him, worrying about what he was doing over there and not understanding what he was doing with her. Don't cut your nose off to spite your face. Don't give in to false truths."

Guru laughed. "She did not know how to secure the bag. She worried about things she did not need to worry about—that was stupid. That dude was paying her rent! You're right, Ramon, sometimes you do need to keep your mouth shut!"

Mini asked, "Why can't she expect flowers and get her rent paid too? What's wrong with her knowing her worth?"

"Her worth to herself or him? Because evidently, he gave her just what she wanted; flowers, now, wasn't that sweet and romantic of him? If he is doing everything for you, why are you worried? That's jealousy. Jealousy leads to envy, and envy leads to hate, and hate leads to murder. He showed you love every day. You can't equate love with flowers."

"Golly, you got a murderous woman out of this, really?" Mini asked.

"Don't get me wrong, like I told you, it's the little things that become monumental. Selfishness leads to jealousy, and jealousy leads to envy and wanting to possess what that person has. And when you can't, it leads to hate. And when you hate, it leads to murdering a person's spirit and tearing them down. Ya dig?"

"Men hate women, that's what it is. They need to stand up and do their part. Why are they always saying what a woman should do?" Mini expounded.

"Men love women. They do not tell women what to do! They just instruct them on how to get what they want."

Mini exploded, "Why in the heck do I need a man to instruct me on what to do or what he wants? I am a grown woman with my own mind. This is ridiculous!"

"Mini, why are you always talking hate when you have the tools to love? The only reason you hate men is that they will not do what you say. You are trying to get them to do things your way, and it does not work. You need a cat!"

"Ramon, I do not hate men. Where are you getting that from? Men have to grow up and take responsibility for their part of the relationship, especially when it does not work. I already have a cat, Sir! What else, you got?"

Mini stood up and stepped toward me, and I took a step toward her. "Tell me, what is your part? State to me, what are you doing? Since you know it all, tell me. How can you make the situation better? Don't tell me about no dude! His guilt does not make you innocent. Now, what is your part of the relationship? What do you do wrong? I'm listening?"

Mini took another step, rolling her neck. "My part in the relationship is to be the solid one, the one that keeps it together when the man bails out. I'm the one holding him and myself down, and I am tired as heck of that! I'm the one who has to build him up and still not get what I need out of the relationship. What I do is what all women do, and that is to be the best of him and me, and still his ass is incognito! Listen to that! Great One!"

"You keep talking about correcting men! You got to correct you! Your universe will not change until you make the change. You got to stop being bitter and be better! You can't think wrong and treat a person right, that's impossible. Do you think I would go around and tell a mother that her son is going to be a bum or drug addict? His mother would say, 'Stop speaking that into my son's life. That's a lie.' It is the same principle.

You cannot keep saying that men are the problem, that's a false truth, that's a lie!"

Guru hugged Mini's shoulder. "Mini, sometimes we as women need to look at our part in the relationship and examine what we might be doing wrong." She laid her head on her shoulder. "Sometimes the Great One says things that are disturbing, but he has a point. I've been guilty of some of those things myself and look at it differently now."

The girls were all chattering at the same time as I stroked my beard. "Simmer down, simmer down, here is another false truth that may clear up some more propaganda! There was a couple that had been dating for a year, and he refused to introduce the young lady to his mother. She felt he was hiding something. Her question was should she demand to go meet his mother? If he doesn't introduce you to his mother, you're not the one that is a false truth because you never know what type of mother the man has. There could be several reasons he is not introducing you to his mother. His mother could be crazy or deranged, or a germaphobe, naw I'm just kidding," I said, giving Sunshine a high-five. "He may feel his mother is inappropriate or embarrassing in some way. He may feel your skin is not tough enough to deal with the dynamics of his mother. Or it could be vice versa. Do not push him on this. Respect his wishes. You are in a relationship with him, and not his mother."

Boonie reacted quickly. "If a man sees me for a year, he better introduce my behind to his mother! I don't care if she has a problem. We all have family members with problems. If we are going to grow, we have to share it all—the good and the bad. I am not so fragile that I can't handle a crazy mother!" She jokingly threw a spitball at me. I ducked, and it missed.

"Good answer, Boonie, but it's not what you do, baby, but how you do it. Anyway, back to the situation at hand. Just because he does not introduce you does not mean that he is not into you. If you knew he loved you, would you care if he introduced you to his mother?"

Sunshine added, "It is not like me to be sweating no man about meeting his mother, he will introduce me when he is ready, but I do understand a woman's need to be cautious about who she is involved with and their background—that includes knowing their family."

"There is nothing wrong with being cautious—you should be. But you ladies need to be more cautious about your behavior and how he reacts to certain things that you do. What makes him want to talk and what makes him not want to listen, that's more important, and that's the truth!"

I glanced toward Boonie with my hand over my heart as if I was serenading her. "If you know he already loves you, what difference does it make if he introduces you to his mother? Because that's the reason why you want to be introduced to her, right? To confirm that he loves you? You sound like you just want him to satisfy your insecurities. I'mma tell you a secret. You can't ever satisfy a woman's insecurities because one insecurity will lead to another."

Sweet Pea revealed her thought. "If you know a woman is insecure, why can't you make her feel secure in her insecurities?"

"Women operate in fear or faith, and you can't let fear creep into your relationship. You must practice faith, and it has to build up and become stronger. You can't satisfy a person's insecurities. That's something that she has to trade in; being insecure for being secure within herself. That's like me saying I'm going to make you happy. Personally, no one can make you happy. Happiness has to start within. Same principle."

Thunder struck with a loud boom and shook the window. "For instance, you first wanted to be introduced to his mother," with a falsetto voice, 'Can I meet your friends now?' Next thing you know, 'You shouldn't be going out with your brother, you know he is a hoe!' Finally, you come home from work at 7pm, then she asks, 'Baby, you get off at 4pm, what took you so long to get home? You need to be home by 5pm!'" These are signs of insecurities that never stop but only grow. These are false truths that you cannot let into your life."

Camelot laughed. "Man, that's the truth. Come on, ladies, y'all know that's right!"

They sat there all rigid. I thought, *even though I gave them concrete evidence, they still seem to have mixed emotions.*

Mini's neck was stiff as a board while she wrestled out an agreeable word like it had a stranglehold on it. "There is some credence in what you are saying. Women can be insecure, and we women should empower ourselves by being happy with ourselves first."

"One sign of insecurity is that it always needs validation. So, what I told you previously in those *Seven Deadly* bullet points, aka Devious Mind, don't use them because they're going to make your life a living hell. But if you use the 7 Hidden Secrets, it can take you to a peaceful, loving, and secure place in your relationship. Doesn't that sound heavenly? On the other hand, your mind has to be renewed on your own. You can lead a horse to water, but you can't make them drink."

"Tell me this Great One?" Mini asked. "If a couple has broken up and they have been apart for at least a year. The man wants to get back with her. How should he approach that situation of them getting back together?"

Boonie glided some lip gloss across her lips. "I can tell you that!"

I sat down in my chair and folded my arms. "Go head Boonie, you got the floor, show me what you are working with!"

Boonie deepened her voice to a man's tone, sat up, and crossed her legs, and with her hand poised as if she was making an imaginary phone call. "Hey, baby, how you doing? I've been thinking about us for a while. I've been doing a self-evaluation, and I thought about all the things that were important to me. The only thing I found in my thoughts that was important was you. Everything that I have done without you was very unsatisfying to me. That led me to realize how much you meant to me."

Boonie changed to her normal voice. "If the woman is silent after this, then all he has to do is allow her to set the terms, and they will be back straight. In a sho nuff good relationship, you know?"

I asked, "Why did they break up in the first place?"

Mini answered, "Because he had 2 to 3 other women, and he spent his money on his family—a lot unnecessarily. He also gambled."

I inquired, "What did she do? Did she do anything wrong?"

"Yeah, he said she talked too loud, hollered at him, cursed him out, and disrespected him in front of his family."

"Who believes that if they stop doing all the wrong things they have been doing to each other and get back together, they will then have a good relationship?"

"I believe they will be alright if he stops doing the things he does, she will stop doing the things she has, done and everything will be fine. I believe they will have a great relationship," Guru answered.

"What you said, Guru, has some truth to it. The truth can be subjective. There are many truths. Some truths are only on the surface, but that is not the underlying problem. The real problem is beyond that. You can eliminate two problems, and here comes three more. You have to understand these are two different people with two distinct minds, and it's contingent on how they may react to the problems when it comes to the bumps in the road. The problems that Mini detailed are not the issue. It is the problems you cannot see that can grow to be unforgivable. The real issue is not that he cheated or that she cursed him out. The real issue at hand is not being able to solve disagreements and problems. This is why it is so important for you to use your Hidden Secrets. They will enable you to overcome any disagreement or dilemma. When you use your Hidden Secrets, it will lead you to the following problem-solving tool, which is patience. Patience will lead you to believe in faith that that person has good intentions toward you, and you must have good intentions toward them. These are the issues you must overcome. When you master these things, then the surface issues will cease to exist. It doesn't matter what the problems are, it's how you solve them.

"Daylight and darkness cannot dwell in the same place. So, let's get rid of all that darkness."

We were all in deep thought, and the quietness in the air allowed us to hear all the little noises in the salon; it even enhanced the raindrops as they tapped on the window in a rhythmic beat.

CHAPTER 6

Tap Dance

A woman that is able to tap into her man,
she will better understand him and how he
functions. It's like driving a car; once you know
how to drive a car, you can navigate where you
want it to go.

"LADIES, GIVE ME a drum roll." They all gave me a fake drum roll. "Turn on the bright lights. Relationships are a lot like tap dancing, and I'm putting on my top hat and lacing up my tap dancing shoes to show you how to tap into a man." With a boyish grin, I asked, "What is humongous but is so small it is invisible?"

Camelot jumped up, "A man's penis!"

We all started cracking up laughing. "Camelot, sit down! The correct answer is a man's ego, silly rabbit." I picked up a rubber band and acted like I was about to pop her with it. She moved quickly like we were in a game of dodgeball. "This brings me to my next lesson—Tap Dance."

"A woman's first entry into a man's mind, body, and soul is through his ego. This is the foundation to tapping into a man. If you really want to be in a healthy relationship, you have to understand a man's ego."

"His whole manhood is based on his ego. It is the most fragile thing in a man. He doesn't handle things or deal with things the same way as you. A woman deals with her emotions through her feelings, and a man deals with his emotions through his ego. That's why it's really hard for him to get over certain things that seem minute to you. Most women feel the things she does for him outweigh the small stuff. But make no mistake, you can do everything he wants, and he may love it, but if you do not take care of his inner feelings, you are going to break him down."

Mini asked, "How is his ego more important than all the things you do for him? What does his ego have to do with that?"

"When you communicate with a man with angry outbursts or demeaning statements, you are tormenting him. Even though it may seem petty to you, it is major to him. Your voice, your words, and your actions have the ability to emasculate him.

"What makes a man tick is his ego. When you are in a relationship, it is important for you to be aware of how you speak to your man. You have to be conscious of what turns a man on and off. If you remain aware, you will have a better chance at a healthy relationship. You can capture a man by his ego like a magnet, and he will be defenseless against your power of persuasion. Your power of persuasion should never be used with aggression because his ego will not allow for it."

"How do you get to a man's ego?" Guru asked.

"A man's ego is how he feels about himself. One of the main ways to get to a man's ego is how you make him feel about himself while he's with you—that means everything to him. A man is helpless against you if you tap into his ego. If you can get into his consciousness and build him up, it is almost hypnotic. You will have him eating out of the palm of your hands. Here's an example. He says, 'Baby, we should go on a vacation to Florida.' You say, 'I don't want to go to Florida. I told you I wanted to go to the Bahamas!' To him, you seem ungrateful, and you are undermining him, which is equal to you breaking his ego. This is what you should say instead, 'Baby, I know you mentioned you want to go parasailing. I heard that the Bahamas has that plus a packaged deal that includes activities and food and drinks. Man, we would have a ball, what do you think? But it's up to you. I'm cool with whatever as long as we get away together.' He will say, 'Let me think about it.' The next day the man is going to say, 'Let's go to the Bahamas!' She says, 'Thank you, baby, that's what I love about you!' See how easy it is to plant a seed when you cater to a man's ego? He is always going to think you know what is best for him. Voila! You get a trip to the Bahamas, the vacation you really wanted all along! You can steer a man in any direction you want him to go because what men really want to do is make you happy."

Sweet Pea turned her chair around and stared at me in a bit of a frenzy. "I got to act all stupid and docile and cater to him like that? We both grown!"

I walked to Sweet Pea and turned her chair toward the ladies, and asked, "Tell me how you would want to talk to your man in this instance?"

Sweet Pea patted her hair in the mirror and turned her lip up, and sighed. "Well, I would just tell him, 'I know you said let's go to Florida for a vacation and that's nice, but I would prefer we go to the Bahamas because we will get more for our money, what do you think about that? I would just be straight up about it!"

"Sunshine, which approach is better, Sweet Pea's or mine?"

Sunshine looked up and laughed softly, "Sweet Pea, I have been happily married a long time, and you do need to know how to work a man's ego. I got to agree with Ramon. He has to believe that you have his best interest at heart. They will move mountains for you when you tap into them that way. Let me just get real with you for a minute; if you tap into him, over time, you don't have to put that much effort into persuading him. It just becomes natural and easy for you to accommodate him and vice versa. No drama!"

I explained, "This is all I'm trying to say. You move your man how you want to move him, depending on how you treat him. A man's whole purpose is to please a woman, but when you affect his ego, then he looks at it differently—you diminish him. Stop trying to make him wrong so you can be right. The only reason you do this is to make him feel small as a man, and that's the worst thing."

I continued. "Listen, ladies, if you get into an argument over the phone and you don't talk for days, but you make the decision not to call him first. He finally calls you, and now you give him a list of expectations and demands. Once you do that, his ego will shrink when you cross that boundary. He will become defensive."

I mockingly hung my head low with a sly grin. "You may think you won, but that is only temporary. Him being a man it is natural for him to strike back, and every time you seem demanding, y'all gonna bump heads. Now that seems simple but check this out. If you and your man get into an argument, you might ask why can't he be the nurturer, the comforter and the better person? The answer to that million-dollar question is he wasn't made that way—you were."

I walked over to Camelot's station and picked up a lace front wig and put it on my head and took a deep breath, and stuck my chest out. Everyone laughed, then I slowly took the lace front off and leaned on Camelot's chair. "It would be best that you call him to nurture him because you are the one with the knowledge and the expertise. That's where your power lies. This is what you should've said when you called him first, 'Baby, I don't want to argue with you. I love you, and I only want the best for you.' Now his ego might jump up, and he might roar like a lion depending on the severity of the situation, but when he comes down from that roar, he will feel like a man. So, when he comes around you, he feels good about himself not inferior, and if he feels good about himself while he is with you, I guarantee you can navigate him any way you want to.

"For instance, there was a couple that had been living together for a while, and he came home at 3 in the morning, and she was sitting there waiting on him looking at the clock. She says, 'Look what time it is!' and starts fussing and hollering. With this approach, these disagreements will definitely keep happening, but I'm going to give you a different approach with a different outcome. If she gets up and cooks breakfast, talks to him like his homie and be sweet to him like his lady, trusts him like she was his wife, then you will see a change. Now if he continues this behavior, she needs to continue doing what she has been doing, which is use her Hidden Secrets, his conscience will not allow him to keep doing it because he will not want to hurt her or change the way she thinks about him. He would not want to do her wrong, and eventually, he will stop. Always remind him how great he is. If you don't understand anything I have said, remember and understand this, what you think about a man means far more to him than what you do for him. It is about taking care of his ego first. He wants to make you happy and feel good about it."

Sunshine added, "A soft word turns away wrath, but a harsh word stirs up anger and sometimes a woman needs to use a feminine touch and a soft word to get to the real issue. If he comes home late at night and you want to know why he keeps doing this, a conversation spoken with a soft and gentle voice with an attitude of love and trust will allow him to feel he can tell you anything."

"Sunshine, we know you did not just agree with that mess! This man just broke this woman's heart and pushed her feelings aside as if they do not matter. He does not have the common courtesy to explain himself, and she is supposed to cook his breakfast and whisper sweet nothings in his ear. Have you lost your ever-lovin' mind?!" Mini passionately spoke out.

"Ain't no way in God's green earth she is supposed to take that approach and expect nothing but a roller coaster ride from a bum," Sweet Pea added.

Sunshine was in the hot seat and stood up and said, "Wait a minute!" Walked over to Mini and Sweet Pea and touched their hands. "You know you all are my girls, and I'm saying this in love. You both need to get your mind right," as she slid her hand back from theirs. "First and foremost, which one of you have ever kept a man for more than a few months? Have your ideologies about men worked out for you? Are either of you in a committed long-term relationship? Do you even know what that means? Relationships are about knowing your position and owning it. He plays a part, and you play a part. If you understand your part better, then success can be yours, but if you don't comprehend where you are going wrong, you are a fool. Only a fool does the same things and expects different results."

Mini pursed her lips tightly and gritted her teeth. "What makes it foolish to be alone? A lot of people start off alone before they get someone. My choice of a man has to suit me. I'm not going to deal with certain behaviors no matter what. If that means being alone, so be it. I'm cool with that."

Sweet Pea's voice trembled with anxiety, "My part is to tell him how I feel, and his part is to communicate back to me, is that not right?"

I walked over to her and said, "Yeah, it is right, but it depends. When communication is being misinterpreted, that's miscommunication, and that is a bad thing. If you communicate and it is not effective, then you know it is not right. The most important thing when you communicate is to understand them, then to tell them how you feel. If you listen to a man, you might not have to tell him how you feel."

Sweet Pea's eyes widened, and they almost appeared bucked while she hunched her shoulders and folded her arms and asked, "How so?"

I rubbed my forehead in sorrow. "Ok, let me make this as clear as possible. You cannot emotionally rule and reign in a relationship. Many times, emotions destroy rationale, and it is best to be quiet and listen. The best time for a female to talk is when she has calmed down. If he comes home at 3 in the morning and you are hot, that is not the best time to talk, you both will not communicate effectively. When a woman is rational, she is the better communicator. When a woman is irrational, she is dumber than a doorknob, but when she is rational, she is the smartest in the room.

"Ok, man, I get it, but that's going to be hard for me," Sweet Pea clamored.

The loud thunder made a quick interruption of our little seminar. We turned and watched the rain pinging the window as water slowly but steadily accumulated up to the curb.

I took a deep breath and wiped the sweat from my brow. "This requires practice. Let me tell you how to test it. If you get so mad and you think you're calm and the man starts getting angry, this will let you know you are not communicating effectively."

Guru was quick to add, "I'm familiar with a man's ego, and it is not hard for me to soothe it. Communication was not my downfall in my marriages. Both of my husbands did not want the divorce at a drop of a dime. I could get either one of them back! That's why they love me so much. But my thing is the choice or caliber of man that's attracted to me. It seems that men with issues always gravitate toward me."

"Your problem is not that you do not know how to tap into your man. It sounds like your problem is you're not navigating the negative and turning it positive in him, but you are allowing the destructive part to overflow. You should not nurture the destructive part because when you do, it grows out of control and ruins the relationship."

Guru sat up to the edge of her seat, "What is the destructive part?"

"Destructive parts could be abuse, addiction, or gambling, and you allow these things because you feel you can deal with them. You cannot compete with many of these types of issues. For instance, this type of issue will override the ego. A man's ego can submit to your will, but addictions have a mind of their own. Do not nurture that part."

Boonie put one hand on her hip and leaned to one side. "My husband would know better than to come in at 3 in the morning, first of all without my permission! My boo is well trained, he knows not to even withdraw money out of the bank without asking first, and that has nothing to do with his ego."

Sunshine said, "Boonie, you are talking about your husband, but he is a different type of man. What is working for your man would never work for my man."

Boonie looked perplexed. "What you talkin' about Sunshine, a man is a man, now I can agree that what works for your man might not work for mine, but what do you mean by type? I have been in a couple of serious relationships, and they were for love. This time, I got into a relationship where the person loved me, and I was in control. My situations were bad at first being in love, but now I've found someone that is good for me. Being in love created a lot of issues for me. If I knew what I knew now then, it probably would be different in those relationships. I did not know anything about no ego—that didn't matter to me. So, what is the difference between my man and yours? "

"Well, there are two types of males, and from what you're saying, you have a Beta male, and mine is an Alpha male."

Camelot's eyes prowled off her notes like a curious cat and looked up, suddenly alert. "What is the difference between a Beta and an Alpha male?"

Boonie laughed. "What difference does that make to you? You don't even like men!"

Camelot sassily said, 'Don't tell me what I like! I have had men before—probably way more than you! It's like this, I like chicken, but I like steak too! I just like steak right now! But if we keep talking about men, I might want to eat a drumstick." she said, giving everybody fist bumps! She looked over at Boonie and said, "Shut up!"

"Ok, ok, everyone. You all seem to have questions on the difference between Beta males and Alpha males, and there is definitely a contrast. Let's discuss the Beta male first. The Beta does not mind doing what you say because he is just thrilled to be a part of a relationship. He likes having you around, so he will do whatever it takes to keep you near. He lacks confidence when it comes to relationships. He tends to be more attracted to aggressive women. Beta males want to be good for the female. If you are looking for a man that is good for you, then you would love a Beta Male."

I popped my collar and said, "Let me give you the details of an Alpha male. An Alpha male wants a woman that is good for him. An Alpha can be egotistical in that he desires a woman that nurtures his imperfections in a certain way to bring out the best outcome for them both. An Alpha male needs a woman that fills the void of what he has needs for. He might need, for example, a good cook because he cannot cook. He might need a woman that can balance his budget because he is not good with numbers. An Alpha male needs a woman that can be a friend to him. A woman is naturally a helpmate, so the Alpha male lets her use her natural ability because naturally, she wants to make things better. If you can understand an Alpha male's imperfections and his needs, then he will give you the world on a silver platter. If you are a woman that wants to be good for a man, then the Alpha male is for you.

"Alpha and Beta can both be equally whorish depending on their level of discipline in that area. Both males are like jobs, but if you love your job, you never have to work another day in your life."

Boonie covered her mouth with one hand and snickered. "Now that you explained the difference, you're darn right my man is a Beta male. Me being with a man is not for love but for convenience, so my preference would be a Beta male because it is about me!"

Sweet Pea asked sharply, "Is my only option to have a beta male? Girl, the answer is no way! I don't want no lip-hanging slouchy foot-dragging man walking around like duh, what you want me to do? My preference is an Alpha male."

"All those who like the Beta male raise your hand?" I asked with a big smile. No hands went up.

Guru said, "My choice would be rough around the edges, with some swag. You know, Alpha males are attracted to me for some reason."

"Telling the truth, I would prefer an Alpha male, but he would have to know my value. It's important to cater to a man's ego. You gave us some good tips," Mini said.

Camelot looked thoughtful and added, "If I decided to be with a man, it would be an Alpha male. There is something about the Alpha I admire."

"It is important for you all to know the different types of males in order to truly tap into them. In the past, some of you might have dated some Beta males, and it worked out great. You meet an Alpha male, and you think you are supposed to treat him like a Beta male, and that's your downfall. You cannot treat all males like Beta males. You have to learn what type of man he is and then treat him accordingly. You see, each type of male requires something different.

"As for you, Sweet Pea, your mouth is not lining up with your actions! You say you don't want a foot-dragging Beta, but that is how you treat all your men. You say you want an Alpha, but you make your relationships all about you. You can never get through to an Alpha that way; you have to make it more about him. The more you make it about him, the more it will be about you because you are a team.

"As for you, Guru, your insecurities are keeping you from completely tapping into an Alpha. You cannot let destructive behavior in to secure the bag. If you are tapping into their ego, you should not get emotional and shut down. It doesn't work like that. You have to continue to plant good seeds, invest in his goodness, and that's where you will get your return. It's a mistake letting your emotions control you and take you out of your comfort zone. Your power of persuasion does not work in anger or fear.

"As for you, Mini, you say you prefer an Alpha male, but you need to change your thoughts about men. You will never tap into an Alpha with force. Your approach is weak because you cannot go toe to toe with an Alpha and expect him to back down. Nothing good will come from that approach. Mini, stop talking about what's wrong with men and start thinking of ways to influence them to do good. "

"As for you, Camelot, you will tap into an Alpha right off because you will start off admiring him and will be a friend, and therefore, have a better relationship. You will be friends a lot longer than anything else.

"As for you, Boonie, if that works for you, at least you know where you are at. A lot of women don't.

"As for you, Sunshine, keep practicing what you preach. If you keep doing that, your husband will be with you for a lifetime. That ain't no joke!"

Mini stepped in front of my chair and tapped her pen on my wrist to get my attention, and stated, "We hear you, but it is not easy with these men out here. You have to guard your heart because they will turn into Dr. Jekyll and Mr. Hyde, especially the ones you are trying to get close to."

The ladies all agreed. "Yeah, that's in the word. The bible tells you to guard your heart!" Boonie shouted out.

"This is something many women do; they use guarding their heart to camouflage their fear." I popped a mint in my mouth from my station. "One time, one of my previous lady friends and I were having a discussion on this very same topic. She was talking about men in general and how every relationship she has had since me was bad."

I made a conceited gesture and wiped my hands as if anyone could compete with me. They softly giggled.

"She explained that she was forced to guard her heart because men tend to flip on her. What she said to me led me to believe she was not guarding her heart but was tapping into a man out of fear. Fear is of the devil, and anything you fear can conquer you. When you expect fear in a relationship, you are always expecting something to go wrong. Unknowingly, you come off as hostile and resentful. Let me explain to you the better alternative, which is faith. Faith allows you to tap into a man through your Hidden Secrets. You cannot nurture and comfort a man in fear. If you have faith, I'm not saying you won't have challenges. Those challenges can be turned around, and you will not be scared of them because you will know what to do when it occurs. What I'm telling you all to do is take something bad and turn it into something extraordinary. I'm not telling you all not to guard your heart when it comes to a maniac that eats nails or drinks ketchup."

Everyone laughed. "I'm telling you all that if you care for somebody, it is ok to let your guard down. But when you let them down and use your Hidden Secrets, you will always have the advantage."

Sweet Pea stated, "Ramon, letting your guard down is not that easy because when someone hurts you, it is hard to forgive and forget. That takes time."

I paused and searched for the right words. "That statement right there should be 10 red flags to a man. If you hear a woman say she has to take one day at a time, that she needs time to get over the pain of your cheating, etc., I would tell him to run the other way. The reason why is because she still has her defensive mechanism up. No way she is going to treat you right because she sees you as an opponent. She is never going to get over it, and she will never be satisfied with what you do. The worst thing a man can do is try to nurture a woman back to mental health. That's her skill set. A woman's natural ability is to make things better, and if you try to be the nurturer, no matter how hard you try, she is going to feel you could do better."

"I'm concerned about one more thing. If you use your Hidden Secrets to tap into a man, how long should you wait to get romantic?" Sweet Pea asked.

Camelot roared with laughter. "Girl, please ask what you really mean, which is how long should you wait to have sex?"

Everyone said, "Yes, yes, that's a good question!"

"To answer your question, Camelot, let nature take its course. There is no specific time in a relationship to have sex. When you feel comfortable, connected, and know enough about him, then that's the time."

"Can we openly ask you some more sex questions?" Boonie wanted to know.

—— ❧ ——

CHAPTER 7

Sex 101

Sex is more than physical—it is psychological.
If you can control the mind, you can control the
body.

"YOU ALL CAN ask me whatever you like. Nothing is off the table!"

Everyone jumped up from their chairs and started doing a sexy dance. They started singing "Do What You Like!" Camelot started twerking her butt cheeks. Mini started rolling her belly!!

"Go Mini, Go Mini" Mini gyrated her hips as she turned around and bent over, and right before she twerked her butt, I made a loud fart sound, "BRAAAP!"

Mini ran over to me and hit me on my shoulder playfully. I grabbed her and hugged her, and said, "You know I love you!"

She said, "I love you too!"

"You are not mad at me like the rest of those dudes, are you?"

"No, because you are my boy!"

"Why, because I don't mean you no harm and my intentions are good?"

"Right!"

"You need to feel the same way about those men as you feel about me. Because you are smart and beautiful. You cannot be selfish and keep all this goodness to yourself. Please promise me you will share this with some, some, some homeless man please old buddy, old pal," I said as she laughed! I kissed her on her forehead repeatedly, and she acted like she was wiping it off as she walked back to her chair. I stuck my tongue out of my mouth and made a little fart sound again— "BRAAAP"—and pointed toward her. They all giggled.

"You said nothing is off the table. Here is my question. Why don't men like to wear condoms?" Boonie asked.

Sunshine quickly answered, "The answer to that question is simple. They don't like how it feels, the same way you don't. They may not want to wear it, but they need to wear one when necessary."

Sweet Pea smoothed her hair. "One reason they may not wear condoms is that they really care about you and want a relationship with you."

Mini jumped in sarcastically. "Sweet Pea, really? You believe that! He cares about how his dick feels!"

Sweet Pea agreed with a smile. "You are right. Sometimes men are pigs when it comes to sex, but I was just trying to give them the benefit of the doubt."

"You girls are both right. If a man likes you enough, he will take a chance on you, and other times, they can be pigs."

Sunshine looked toward me. "My client asked me this question, and I want you, Oh Great One, to answer it since you are a man (heeheehee), and we want a man's perspective. She asked if her man does not have an orgasm, does that mean she is bad in bed?"

Guru shouted out. "Her stuff must be garbage."

Laughter rolled over the room.

"That's a complex question because there could be several reasons. Sometimes, a man withholds his orgasm, so he can please you, and once his orgasms keep going up a few times, then it becomes difficult for him to have one. Or he could have health issues like erectile dysfunction, medication, and a lot of stuff."

"Great One, this a question that a lot of my girlfriends ask me. How can you ask a man to be tested for STDs without freaking him out?" Guru asked.

I rubbed my chin. "Hmm... that always seems to be a problem. Tell him you want to do sexual things to him, and you don't want to have a conscience about it. Nothing should be off-limits. Explain to him you don't want to have to hold back on anything."

"Good answer, Great One!"

Camelot asked, "Does a man have G-spots? If so, where are they?"

"You little pussycats are getting too deep, but this is good, so let me educate you. Yes, men have spots. I'm not sure I would use the phrase G-spots to describe them. There are certain spots on a man that can make his orgasm more intense; it just depends on the man and what turns him on. Some men like you to suck or bite his nipples, pull on his scrotum sack or finger his perineum (spot between the scrotum and rectum) or anus as he comes."

"Yeah, a man's erogenous zone is in his anus!" Guru stated.

"Be careful with that anus, don't be digging for gold."

Sunshine grimaced and said, "Oh, that's a nasty picture you just painted."

Mini asked, " Let me ask you this. Why do men pressure women for anal sex? Don't they know that hurts? Then they get all offended if you tell them let me stick a dildo in your behind so you can see how it feels!"

Everybody shook their heads. "Whoa, Mini, you off the chain!"

I put my hand over my mouth, trying to hide my smile. "First of all, men like a variety of things. Anal sex gives you more options, so everything won't be so one-dimensional. If you are willing to have anal sex with your man and it hurts, there are ways to go about it. There is numbing cream you can buy to stop the pain. You rub it on the anus, and he lubricates himself. It lasts for about 10 minutes, and it makes it much easier for you all to have sex that way."

Camelot immediately asked, "Well, if a man likes to have sex that way, does that mean he is gay?"

My legs were getting a little tired. I leaned back on my station and folded my arms. "No, because he is with a woman, and anything a man does with a woman most definitely means he does not want to do that with a man, period. Unless he wants you to use an object such as a dildo in his anus, then that's a horse of a different color!"

"Just like you are a lesbian, and they like oral sex, right?"

"Yeah," Camelot replied.

"Every woman in here probably likes oral sex, but that doesn't make them gay."

Boonie added, "Oh my, no oral sex is a deal-breaker, baby! Since we talking about being gay, my question is if a man wants a threesome with another man, is he gay?"

"That old beta male wants a threesome?" Camelot asked.

"This is just a question. Mind your business!"

"Back to the question at hand, it depends on how he wants the threesome. If, for instance, he wants his woman and a male friend to screw each other, he probably is not gay. But if he and the man are screwing and you are there to watch, then he is gay. If he has you and another female getting down with each other while he participates, then he is not gay—he is a stone cold freak! Some people are into that. They are called swingers. Stay away from threesomes! Because once you start, it is on the table."

Mother Nature did a thundering clap to remind us she was still in the midst—the noise startled us. I continued. "When you let somebody in the relationship, it stirs up all kinds of feelings and creates problems. It can initiate all types of emotions such as love, hate, or jealousy, and that could be difficult to shut off. This type of sexual appetite is hard to curb because you want it more and more. It can cause you to become a thrill-seeker, which, in turn, can open up doors that lead to immorality."

Camelot was quick to say, "Ain't nothing wrong with threesomes. Variety keeps it spicy, right?"

Sunshine weaved into the conversation, "No way! First of all, I would never do a threesome period, especially with another woman. If I did do a threesome, it would have to be with another man (heeheehee)."

"Sunshine, you silly!" Sweet Pea replied in a chipper voice.

"Moving right along, what's the next question?" I asked as I walked to the water cooler to get a cup of water.

Guru asked, "You know what, tell me this? When you put on beautiful sexy lingerie to spice it up, why do men act like they don't care?"

"For some men, a simple t-shirt with nothing on under it is all he needs to get him going. Most times, ladies, as hard as it is to hear, they could care less about what you wear to bed but about what is underneath. You often buy sexy lingerie for yourselves because you think it is pretty and you like how it makes you feel."

"Naw man, dudes ask me all the time to send them pictures of myself in sexy lingerie," Sweet Pea cut in.

"Well, his sexual appetite may have something to do with it. Some men might like strippers and want you to wear sexy lingerie because they like eroticism. Here's a helpful hint: if you wear sexy lingerie, tell him to make it rain."

"So, are you saying get paid for it?" Sweet Pea asked.

"Yes!"

"Don't that take the romance out of it?"

"Naw, I'm just kidding."

Mini said her friend asked her, "Why do men come home complaining all the time about how you don't look sexy? They say you look a mess, your hair is all wrapped up, you have on my old t-shirt and sweatpants. I want you to look sexy, and you don't. What do I do to up my sex appeal for my man?"

"Well, there are different types of men that have different things that appeal to them sexually. Sexy is a mindset. If a man genuinely cares for you, he's going to care for you inside out. Sexiness comes from within. If you have to cover it up with material things, there's something wrong in that relationship. When a man tells you that something is wrong on the outside with you, then there is something wrong with him on the inside. He is using that to justify his wrongdoing, such as going out to a strip club, cheating, or having a baby out of wedlock. Sexiness is not the problem. He is phony as a $3 bill. You need to ask him what his angle is, and is there something we need to talk about? As for upping your sex appeal, ask him what is sexy to him about you? Once he tells you, then you will know exactly what to do to increase your sex appeal."

Sunshine took a sip of juice she had brought in with her that morning and said, "Yeah, Ramon, you are right. My husband is not for all that lingerie. What he finds sexy is me wearing one of his sleeveless t-shirts and boy shirts that show off what he says are my best assets. That's what is sexy and appealing to him."

Boonie chimed in, "We all know what Camelot's best asset is!" Everybody laughed.

With a low tone of confidence, Camelot responded, "Don't hate!" as she threw her head back in laughter.

"My sister told me this, and I cannot for the life of me understand what the problem is," Mini said as she huffed out her breath. "She said I do not mind oral sex, but I do not want my man to ejaculate in my mouth. She was wondering why he had to do that?"

I pulled my ponytail back and secured it with a new rubber band, and said, "Understand part of the full orgasm for a man is ejaculating, and if you pull away before he finishes, he does not get that full experience which cannot be at all satisfying. How would you feel if your partner pulled back just as you were about to have your orgasm? That would be very frustrating. There is a mental and physical intensity that he gets from coming in your mouth. Would you want to deny your man his full capacity of pleasure?"

"Ooookay!" Mini said patiently.

Sweet Pea grabbed her pencil and pad from her station and walked over by Sunshine, and lowered her eyelids with a thought, "Why do men keep asking me if I squirt? What does that mean?"

"Good question! From my experience, here's my theory. Squirting is really female ejaculation."

"Women ejaculate? Are you talking about women's vaginal juice?" Sunshine asked with a scowl.

"No, it is actually a fluid that comes from the urethra. There are two holes, one for your pee and the other for this fluid. It does not come from the vagina. When you squirt, it comes from a gland called the vestibular near your urethra. This gland has the same type of sensation as the clit, and when stimulated, the squirt can come from both holes. It usually happens when you stimulate the woman's G-spot and a woman has an orgasm. When you are highly aroused, it helps lubricate everything. It also has a sweet taste."

"How do we tell the difference between vaginal fluid and this gland you are talking about?" Sweet Pea asked.

"Because the gland squirts out like pee and is sensitive like the clitoris. If you rub it a certain way with friction, it starts to protrude, and you can feel it, and then it starts squirting.

In order to experience this, tell your man to put just the head of his penis in the vagina and tilt it upward and stroke back and forth to press against the gland and let him keep fooling around until he finds that spot. If that doesn't work, let him try his finger instead. It is half an inch into the vagina up toward the stomach. The gland has a rough texture that feels like grooves. Gently rub your finger toward the clit repeatedly, and that should do it."

"I love when they squirt. I'm a squirter!" Camelot excitedly said.

Sunshine turned away with a muttered plea, "That's TMI, please stop Camelot!"

Guru quickly picked up her pen and pad and started writing and said, "That is some good stuff, and I'm taking notes for later tonight! If you know what I mean. I will give y'all the low-down tomorrow."

Sweet Pea glanced up from her notepad, "Now that you have explained it, I'm a squirter too because that be happening to me a lot when I have sex."

"Some of my friends have told me they have never had an orgasm with their man and that they cannot have an orgasm with penile penetration but only orally. What's up with that?" asked Sunshine.

"It's easy for me either way, I'm orgasmatic!" Mini volunteered.

"A man has to have good technique," Guru explained.

"First of all, you need to share this with your friends. They have to find out what they like. If they don't know what they like, how can they instruct their men? That may be an issue they need to deal with. These ladies may have low energy. They need to find out what turns them on about a man. Regarding the second part of your question about only having orgasms with oral sex. One of the reasons is they could have a tilted pelvis. It could be tilted up, and that would be normal, but when the pelvis is tilted down, it might be difficult to reach that erogenous spot. My suggestion is to place a wedged or triangular pillow they can buy specifically for this under the buttocks. That way, it's easier to find her G spot. So, you have to find out what turns you on to reach a certain body temperature to trigger the mind to activate that organ to function properly. The first time a woman has sex, and it is orally, and her clitoris gets stimulated that way; that projects into the mind, it triggers that part of the brain and stays there forever, and therefore, she is unable to have an orgasm any other way."

"Is that the reason a man cannot have an orgasm orally if he had vaginal sex first?" Mini asked.

"No, it is not!"

"So, if you have oral sex with a man and he never has an orgasm, does that mean you're lousy?"

"Yes, that means you are lousy if he does not ever have one!"

We all filled the room with laughter.

"Alright, here's another helpful hint. If you want to be better at that, you have to learn where a man's pleasure zone is on his penis. It's right underneath the head of the penis. That part of a man's penis is similar to a woman's clitoris because that is where all the nerve endings are." Everyone's ears were plastered to my every word.

Mini stopped writing and asked, "Do you mean just lick my tongue on the backside of the head of his penis, and that should do it?"

"No, my little pumpkin heads. You need to put your entire mouth on the head of the penis and lick and suck in an up and down motion, not the entire shaft, just the head and right underneath. By the way, this detailed information is for married people!"

Guru slightly slid down in her chair and held her pen to her chin, "How do I get my man to have oral sex with me?"

"First of all, make sure it ain't stankin!"

"Right, don't nobody want fish for dinner. Make sure the coochie is fresh and clean!" Camelot loudly exclaimed.

I laughed in amusement, "A fresh furry burger swallowed down with some sweet lemonade!

"This is only for somebody you have a connection with and trust. First of all, you need to use your Hidden Secrets—nobody can get past that. You can put these training wheels on him and start it out slow. In the middle of foreplay, when he rubs your vagina, take the hand he rubs your vagina with, and rub it on your nipple. Then bring his head gently to your nipple and see if he sucks it. If he does, he will do it, it's ago!

"I'm telling you this because I want you to be able to use your Hidden Secrets physically, mentally, and spiritually on your mate. This is about winning in every aspect of your relationship. Everybody likes a nice girl, but men have sexual appetites that need to be fulfilled as well. You know the saying, 'Every man wants a lady in the street and a freak in the bed.'

Sweet Pea tapped on her desk as she raised an issue of concern, "This is a good one for you, Great One. What if your man's technique in the bedroom is less than adequate. How do you tell him without offending him?"

The conversation had gotten deeper than expected, but it was all good. We had come too far to turn back now.

"Sweet Pea, my dear, you can talk to him in the third person. For example, my girlfriend and I were talking, and she was telling me that she was unsatisfied with her dude. So, I asked her what the problem was. She said he has sex like a jackrabbit—really fast. I like it very slow and easy. So, I tried to guide him to slow down. He will slow down for a minute, then he speeds up again. How can I tell him this without hurting his feelings? Like myself, I like it fast, but when you go slow, that's when it really feels good, oh my God! When you go slow, that makes me have an orgasm. So, I told her to grab his hips and direct him on his speed and rotation. If your man has been the jackrabbit, you really have told him indirectly."

"How do men feel about toys in the bedroom?" Boonie asked.

"It depends on if the man is included or excluded in the act itself. If he is included and he is participating in the act, then he might feel ok about it. But if you are off doing your own thing and he is not included, then he might feel some type of way about that. He will believe that he does not need to be there and does not serve any purpose. As for women using toys in masturbation, this comes from my experience and talking to many, many women who have indulged in this type of behavior, the result is it deadens the nerve endings because the toy operates at such a high velocity, the vagina becomes overstimulated and becomes unresponsive with human penetration over time. In other words, physically, it's unhealthy."

Sunshine quickly commented, "If that's the case, we won't be using no toys because I don't want to be dead down there. I want to feel an orgasm when my man penetrates me!"

All the ladies said, "We are with you on that one!"

"This was a question my girlfriend asked me. How can she initiate her man to talk dirty to her? I said, 'What the heck you? Don't know how to talk to your man in the bedroom? Just tell the chump to talk dirty to you.' But what do you say, Great One?" Guru asked.

I leaned back in my chair with ease and smoothly responded, "Maybe it might be dumb to you, but there is no dumb question. Just tell her to tell him to let her know what he is about to do next during foreplay. When he responds, act like you enjoy it. Then you ask him again what are you going to do next, then tell him you want him to say more, and he might say, 'I'm going to suck on your nipples and bite on them, and when he hears how pleasurable that sounds to you and that you love it, he won't mind doing it."

"Which do men like better—hand jobs or blow jobs?" Mini asked.

"You can make both equally pleasurable if done correctly. Men probably would prefer oral sex over a hand job."

"I need to be well-rounded, so can you tell us what's the proper way to give a hand job in case this sweet girl wants to go in that direction?" Camelot asked.

"Sweet girl, you already know how to give a hand job!" Boonie laughingly commented.

"Shut up, let Ramon just tell us!

"All right, so one thing not to do is start at the base. I've already explained to you a man's most sensitive spot is at the top of his penis. So if you lubricate your hand or his penis, be sure to squeeze the top with a constant motion and make sure that your hand strokes the back of the head. You can go down a couple of times, but always come back up to the head of the penis, squeezing gently."

Mini said, "Answer this, Ramon. When you role-play, why do men accuse you of cheating? They ask where you get that from when you are only trying to spice it up a bit!"

"That's a tricky situation right there because we are used to somebody doing something one way. Then you change it up with something new, then we automatically start wondering where they got it from. If we thought that they got it from another man or woman, even if we like what they are doing, we will probably reject it initially. We don't want them bringing nothing in the house from some other person. We have to communicate a little bit better, so our significant others won't be insecure about it."

"Do you think it's good to role play?" Sunshine asked.

"Now, as far as role-playing, it can be healthy or unhealthy. Just say you role play as a stripper, and your man thinks that you subconsciously want to be one. Therefore, that makes him believe that it's ok to like strippers because you display that type of sexual behavior. That could open up the door for him to desire to see the real deal. The healthy side is you can bring something new and stimulating to your sex life. I would just keep the role-playing free of strippers, prostitutes, and things of that nature."

"Does an orgasm feel different or better for a man if he loves a woman or if he just having non-committal sex?" Sweet Pea asked.

"Sex feels better when a man is in love with the woman because you make love to not just her body, but to her mind and soul. On the other hand, it can feel good with someone you don't care about because you are just focused on the sex and not the other person and their feelings and how you feel about them."

Mini sat up promptly. "I know this is a question that most women have probably had at one point in their life, and that is why doesn't a man like to cuddle after sex?"

"After sex, a man loses his sexual desire for you momentarily. That's when a man knows exactly how he feels about you. When he loses his sexual desire, it makes him want to create space between you two temporarily, not forever, only for a short time. He may love you and want intimacy with you, but at that moment, he loses sexual energy, so he may not want to cuddle. I'm not saying that he won't because some guys will."

Sweet Pea waved her arms wildly, in a hurry to speak. "You said that at that moment, he will know exactly how he feels about you—explain that."

"What it means is at that moment it becomes crystal clear to a man what he likes about you and what he doesn't. It reveals the illusion of lust versus love."

Mini stated, "As a woman, some of us require intimacy, a sense of connection and bonding, especially after sex. He don't have to do it all night, but right afterward, it kind of gives you a feeling of security."

"Think about that. A woman wants security. Security means comfort to her. That's what she looks for. Why do you think women have a big problem with being insecure? Basically, what I'm telling you, my little blueberry muffins, is that if you use your Hidden Secrets, you can get all the post-sex cuddling you want!"

As the ladies chatted amongst themselves, Camelot asked, "Inquiring minds want to know, Ramon, what type of women do you like?"

CHAPTER 8

—— ❧ ——

Turning the Tides

You have to take lemons and make lemonade.
How to turn a bad situation and make it into
a good one. This is a skill that is important for
a woman to have because it is never too late
to turn the situation around. Take a mess and
make something marvelous out of it.

I LIFTED MY eyes toward the ceiling, and a long silence hung in the room. "There is no certain type. She doesn't have to look or dress a certain way. She does not have to have any special requirements. If I meet a girl, and we have good chemistry, then that's the one. All she needs to know is how to tap into those Hidden Secrets."

"What a minute! You need someone compatible with you. Tapping into a man is brilliant, but couples have to like the same thing. Is that right or not?" Sweet Pea's voice went up an octave.

"Not necessarily. The reason why you tap into a man is to know how to fix a problem. I'm going to use a car analogy for a relationship. Say you buy a car, care for the car, keep it clean, and don't drive recklessly, but when something goes wrong, you don't know what to do to fix it. Now, it's just sitting there. At some point, you have to get another car. Then you get another one, and it breaks down, and now you have the same problem. Even if it's something simple as a flat tire, you can't drive it where you need to go. You have to know how to be the mechanic in the relationship."

"So, I'm saying it's not compatibility that will keep you together, but it's how you handle disagreements and problems. You have to be a problem solver. So, I'm showing you how to solve any problem that comes up. You are certified in that area. Use those Hidden Secrets. You won't fail in faith! You can fix any problem, but you have to believe because some problems cannot be avoided."

"Okay, you told us already about being the comforter and the fixer. Now to tell me again why?" Sweet Pea asked.

"You are the nurturer. It's like this: a man takes something heavy upstairs. You probably could do it, but he's better equipped than you. You are more equipped than him when it comes to intelligence in solving problems. You are made to make anything better and add to it no matter what. Your reasoning is unmatched. We all know a woman can take a few items and make a meal or take a house and make it a home. Take a man and produce a child."

"So, you're saying even if we only have a little in common or no compatibility, as long as we can solve disagreements and problems that will keep us together?" Guru asked.

"Yes, I'm saying that compatibility will not keep you together if you can't solve problems. All the online dating sites with their compatibility scores will not mean anything because the minute you get into it with each other, you find out you don't like each other at all! And don't have a clue of how to fix it!"

"I'm going to ask you a question about how many of you we're compatible with someone, and you liked the same things, did the same things, and had the same morals. What about the relationship you were the most sexually compatible with? I bet y'all are not with them now. Why? Because you could not solve the problems or disagreements. Does that answer your question?"

Nobody said a word, and I continued. "In a relationship, you don't have to have nothing in common, but you all can love each other in such a mature way, it brings you closer together instead of your differences tearing you all apart. That creates a mature, everlasting love. Now, I'm not saying don't date a person that doesn't have anything in common with you, but in the long run, you're going to need a lot more than just that. Stop saying you want a man like this, and you want a man like that; that's nonsense. You want a man that you can understand because you have tapped into him. That makes for good chemistry."

"What is good chemistry?" Guru asked.

"Good chemistry is when two people get out of rhythm, they can fall back into sequence and bring everything back into harmony. That means patience, understanding, and self-lessness. You have to make a sacrifice. The only way for that to happen is to tap into your Hidden Secrets and use your power of persuasion, so he can be attentive to you."

"I never understood being a fixer, but I can say that's what we are. We are mechanics of life—we solve problems," Camelot said.

"Camelot, tell me about one of your experiences with men in a relationship, at least one."

"She doesn't even like men. How is she going to give a comment about a man?" Boonie asked.

"What do you know about me?" Camelot fired back, putting her hands on her hips and giving the girls round circle finger snaps. "I have had more dick than all of y'all!"

"You are a slut!" Guru said jokingly.

"Shut up, Guru. It takes one to know one!"

"One time, it was this guy that I really loved. He called me over to his house one evening, and he had this female over there, and it took me by surprise. He invited me in, and he asked me if I would be interested in a threesome with her. You want me to, what? Hecky Naw! But he had this effect on me, ooh wee. This was my little grammar school crush since I was eleven years old. I was feeling like this; since you can't beat them, join them. I'm thinking, well, if he sleeps with her, then why not sleep with her too? We slept with the chick, and I enjoyed it, but at the same time, that hurt me. This is what made it very bad for me—the girl came up pregnant. Man, that just devastated me. I told him to tell her to get an abortion, he said he did not believe in that because it was against his religion. But here's the kicker, when I got pregnant, he allowed me to get one. He said that the reason he let me get an abortion was that he was not sure it was his. From that point on, trusting men became an issue for me. I always put my guard up when it comes to men. Women became more trustworthy to me."

"We definitely can understand how you would become distrustful of men after a story like that," Sunshine quietly responded.

"Not trusting men is a defensive mechanism."

"You're right, Ramon," Camelot replied.

"He tapped into you physically when you should have tapped into him mentally. In some observant way, he already saw that high sexual energy in you and that you were a freak. People can sometimes see things in individuals that they might not even see in themselves. Water always finds its own level. The difference between you and her is that you tapped into what he desired, and she tapped into what was required. What is required is what his needs are, and you find that out through your Hidden Secrets and your intellect. Tapping into him mentally means tapping into his imperfections. You're the fixer, and you fix his imperfections."

"Can a man be fixed?" Camelot asked.

"Yes. That's a woman's job to fix whatever is broken. This is a natural ability a woman has—it is part of her."

"What if a man does not allow you to fix anything? Or if you try to fix something he thinks you are emasculating him?"

"If you are fixing the things that need to be fixed, he will never feel like that. That is not how a man functions. Now, if you are in there trying to fix something that is not broken and are trying to be controlling, he might not accept your help. Let me straighten y'all out on this. Get your pencils and pads. The difference between fixing and controlling is that fixing is when someone needs your help, and controlling is when you just take the situation and use it to your advantage to strengthen your position and to weaken theirs for leverage. You don't have to fix everything. You can coach them into fixing it. Give them the information they need to help and motivate them and bring out their creativity to assist them to be their better selves."

"Did you call Camelot a freak earlier?" Sweet Pea asked.

"In everything that was said, is that all you heard? Freak!"

"No. We talked about fixing imperfections and not trying to control a man with leverage, so you can boss him around because he is overly dependent on you. Is that right?" Sweet Pea said as she brushed her knuckles off on her shirt.

"You said women should tap into men's imperfections. Is it wrong for someone to choose someone for their perfections?" Camelot asked.

"Normally, we admire people for their perfection. We marvel at their excellence. But no matter how great they are or how compatible they are with us, if we don't see flaws and where we can comfortably fit in their life, we will only idolize them from a distance because we are afraid of the unknown. Whether you know it or not, people dislike you for your perfections, not your imperfections. A lot of times, ladies, when other women hate on you, it is not about something you are flawed in. It is always something that is unique about you."

"No wonder they be hatin' on me, it's because I'm gorgeous!" Sweet Pea said, swaying back and forth in her chair.

Guru jumped to her feet. "This makes sense now!"

The clouds continued to roll and make the sky dark with rain, but the excitement and expectation in the room remained.

"This is why when it comes to men, you are drawn to their imperfections—where you can be the nurturer and fixer. And if you don't believe this, just look into the mirror, and in about five seconds, you are going to find something you need to fix. Imperfections activate the nurturing part of you."

Pointing her finger in the air as if it was a light bulb moment, Sunshine asked, "Is that the reason why all the ladies gravitate to the bad boy?"

"You are absolutely correct! When a bad boy is present, he is the most dangerous man in the room! Because all his imperfections show, he attracts women like bees to honey."

"This really shed some light for me. Before we had this discussion, my mind would have gone in a whole different direction, Great One. Being a fixer and a nurturer of somebody's imperfections would not have worked for me. I would have said, 'I'm not submitting and fixing nobody, and nurturing is for kids!' You could have never made me understand that nurturing a man is the same as nurturing anybody else.

My thinking would have been that nurturing a man is different from nurturing a kid, parents, or a friend," Camelot concluded.

"Camelot, that is great you understand that! Let me explain why some women might not understand. Some women will perceive a man in a different light than everyone else—as though he does not need encouragement and comfort like any living human being. He specifically needs that from his woman. You will need to stop thinking that all men are painted with the same brush. You have to believe in something greater than yourself for your mindset to change. You have to plant positive seeds in yourself regarding men, so when your mate does come along, you will be able to look at your mate with good intentions in your heart."

Camelot talked with a pinch of faith, "What I did notice is when we get with women, sometimes they plant seeds in your head, and it will manifest. Especially when they have been hurt, they will transfer that negative picture to you. You see what they see."

I grabbed the towels near my station and started to fold them. "Women compartmentalize things they dislike, and it colors how they feel about you, and it is often not completely or fully true. Especially if a woman perceives you have rejected her. Something insignificant to a man can become monumental to a woman based on her emotional perception of the situation. Certain episodes will be an emotional trigger for a woman, and it may seem insignificant to a man, but it is a big deal to her, and he doesn't even understand what the big deal is, but she has not forgotten it."

Outside the window, the rain appeared to be slowing down a pace. "What seems cloudy and distorted will break through with sunlight because there is an antidote for those triggers. Darkness is like poor perception, and light is like Hidden Secrets, and they both cannot dwell in the same place. The antidote is your Hidden Secrets and your faith that leads you to a different mindset. It breaks you out of being a prisoner of poor perception."

"Man, what a difference a day makes. If I knew then what I know now, things would have been different," Camelot commented.

"So, what are you saying? Are you trading a furry burger in for a polish sausage?" Boonie asked with a disbelieving expression on her face.

They all bent over in laughter, trying to catch their breath.

"It does not matter what your sexual preferences are as long as you understand what I'm saying, ya dig?" I replied.

They were all whispering and comparing notes. "Now that you ladies understand your Hidden Secrets better. Alright, Sweet Pea, let me ask you something. Tell me about a relationship you experienced and what you would have done differently based on what you've learned."

Sweet Pea closed her eyes momentarily and leaned her head back on her chair. "Ok... umm, I was dating this guy, and I had been feeling him for a while. We, at times, seemed to really complement each other. He was good-looking, funny, a nice dresser, had his own business, great in bed—just the full package. Unfortunately, I let my insecurities get the best of me. One day we had friends over, and he was teasing me with my special nickname, and I told him to stop more than once. It brought about an embarrassing feeling, and he continued to taunt me about what I was going to do to stop him. Before I knew it, I had grabbed a fork and jabbed him in the hand."

Sunshine stopped her and said, "Girl, what was wrong with you?"

"Well, I was not in a good place with this man, Ok! There were several other incidents where I threatened to burn him with hot curling irons in front of his daughter. I got mad and called the police on him for no reason and texted him 10 times in one night. After we broke up, I still had access to his voice-mail, and I called this girl that he seemed to be interested in. I was determined to block it before it got started. I stalked him and followed him to her house, and waited for him to leave. I rang the doorbell, and she came outside, and I confronted her, and we got into a fistfight."

"Sweet Pea, you know you're psychotic right?" Camelot stated.

"My mind was in an emotional tailspin, Camelot. I had become a slave to my emotions. Several of my girlfriends had been putting a bug in my ear about him, and this allowed them to feed my insecurities because of my fear that something could go wrong. Looking back, there were people in my ear who were afraid of something going right. You know the saying, misery loves company. Man, I now know my actions were so wrong. I realize now I was not using my Hidden Secrets and was walking in fear and not in faith. Instead of using comfort,

I was using conflict. Instead of my intellect, I used ignorance. I definitely had a devious mind, and I was operating in all seven of them."

"This is deep, but what was the nickname you jabbed him about?" Guru asked with her jaws stretched wide with a grin.

"He called me Monkey heeheehee."

"I would have slit his tires. Just kidding!" Guru sniggled.

I stood in the middle of the floor and barked out a comment. "See, you talked yourself out of a great man the way you described him. Man! Jealousy is like a fire that burns out of control. A contentious woman is worse than a private investigator. We get so caught in our emotions that we become more loyal in how we feel than what is right. Right is wrong, and wrong is right. If you have the same mindset, you will inevitably do the same thing over and over again. Let me tell y'all something and listen good, don't ever, ever let no woman tell you about your man and how bad he is. Because no matter what is going on in your relationship, you have the ability to turn it around. That's what Hidden Secrets are all about. It is about overcoming challenges between a man and a woman."

"Mini, you're next. Whatcha got?"

Mini stretched and rolled her shoulders like she was getting ready for a prizefight. "Well, where do I begin? I have had so many disappointments. While listening to you, I remembered a relationship I had with this guy. What I thought a man should be like was my pastor, my co-worker's husband, my father, and I had this fantasy of what a real man was. Whatever this guy would do was never good enough. For instance, when he would come in late from a party, I would tell him, 'I guarantee you my co-worker's husband would never come home this late.' I would expect him to go to bed at a certain time and tell him my pastor tells us he always goes to bed early because the early bird gets the worm. If he and I had a disagreement and he did not understand me, then I would withhold sex. When something became broken in the house, and if he did not fix it, I would tell him, 'My father always knew how to fix things, why don't you?'"

"You were trying to control him. Did you all have a lot of arguments?" Sunshine asked.

"Yeah, we did. I was angry because he did not do what I needed him to do. We would have a tototoe blowout. This is the way I thought I should be, and I wanted to make him understand my value and my worth. I always thought that men did not have good intentions, and if they did these things like the fantasy I had built in my mind, then it would be proof they had the right intentions. But I realize from this discussion that if I want them to have good intentions, then I need to have good intentions toward them. I should never compare a man to another man because now I know that is tearing him down. I was trying to control him to keep him from hurting me. I was emasculating this man. It turned out bad, and he left. What I learned from talking to you all is that I should have used my Hidden Secrets to build him up. It was all about me, and I should have made it about him, and in the end, it would have made it about us."

My arms were folded as I listened to Mini's surprising revelation. "You're right, Mini. When you tap into who they are, you have to accept them for who they are. When you don't, you are saying you're not good enough for me. That is controlling and mean-spirited. Instead of arguing with him about who he is not, you have to help him be the best he can be. You can't be emotional and egotistical and have a dual personality. You can't play a woman and man's role at the same time. You have to be one or the other."

"That's a transgender!" Camelot shouted.

I was humored by her little analogy. "Hmmm, you might be right, Camelot, you're on to something!"

"Hey, Guru, give us the scoop. Good gobbledygook!"

"Ramon, you are such a cornball!" Sunshine said with a bubbly laugh.

Guru spoke with words of confession as if she was at an altar. "My relationship problem was with a married man. He was a smooth talker, and he swept me off my feet. It was a passionate relationship, and what he handed out, I was addicted to it. One day out of the blue, he stopped calling and texting me. At the time, it was incomprehensible why he would do me that way. Yet, before today's discussion, if he had called me, I would have gone running right back to him. After talking to you all, I now realize that I was putting stock into something that I would never get a return on. Nine times out of ten, a man is not going to leave his wife. You cannot use your Hidden Secrets in the dark because you are not allowing yourself to experience the light."

"Yeah, you right, Guru, because you closed yourself off, and you were willingly staying in the dark. A situation like this has a mind of its own. You are helping him stay married."

"How so, Great One?"

"You are helping his wife out by doing everything she won't and making it easy on her and easy for him to stay with her. He gets you to do the stuff he is tired of her doing. When he gets with a few outside women, and he goes back to his wife, she seems so much more refreshing. He thinks to himself, *"Oooh Wee, I got such a good wife!"*

"Just out of curiosity, why do you think the married man just stopped calling Guru?" Sunshine asked.

"External only lasts so long..."

CHAPTER 9

Beauty Is Only Skin Deep

It is not your looks but your outlook that dictates your outcome. It is better to work on the inner beauty. It is better to work inside out.

"...BUT INTERNAL LASTS a lifetime, which leads me to say beauty is only skin deep."

The ladies huddled up close together and sang in synchronized harmony. "She may be fine on the outside, but so untrue on the inside, Beauty's Only Skin Deep Yeah, Yeah, Yeah, Oooh Yeah," a song by The Temptations.

I belted out, "Give a big applause to the Tempting Cupcakes," As we all laughed.

"Quiet, please! Ok, now! Let me explain what "beauty is only skin deep" means by role-playing. Camelot and Sunshine, come over here by me. Each one is going to play a different role. Camelot is going to play the undercover freak. Sunshine is going to play the goody-two-shoes."

Camelot frowned and said, "Why I got to play the freak? Sunshine has been married a hundred years. You know she is a bigger freak than me!"

"Camelot, don't be lettin' my secrets out the bag. Freaks got to stick together…shhhhh!!!

I looked down at her patent leather pants and said, "Who got on the coochie cutters?"

"That would be me!" Camelot said with a big smile bouncing her butt in the air.

We were all rolling with laughter. I said, "Let's get serious!"

"One of you needs to describe Camelot's appearance, and another needs to describe Sunshine's. Any volunteers?"

All of them anxiously raised their hands. "Ok, Guru, you can describe Camelot and Sweet Pea, you can describe Sunshine."

Guru leaned back to one side, crossed her legs, and looked Camelot over in detail.

"Camelot has on a white top with her nipples showing and black patent leather pants. They are tight in her crotch and around her butt."

Camelot squinted her eyes, giggled, and tossed her blonde hair over her shoulders.

Sweet Pea sat up in her chair. "Okay," as Sunshine widened her eyes in anticipation. "She has a curly fro, no makeup, a little lip gloss, and black slacks with a black t-shirt and a black smock."

"One day, a client asked me, 'How can I attract an upstanding guy?' I told her it was going to be hard for her because she always had on her "hoe uniform." She was shocked and asked me what I meant by that. I went on to inform her that how you dress can determine the kind of attention you get. For instance, look at how Camelot is dressed in tight and revealing clothes, long bright colored hair, a lot of makeup, etc. This is a way to grab the opposite sex's attention, and it is not always in a good way."

Catching my breath to clear my throat, "Uhh... umm... here is the scene, and there are two ladies in my vision. Pretend you two, Camelot and Sunshine, are the ladies talking to each other. Here comes the big bad wolf, which will be me. The big bad wolf is going to be attracted to something visually appetizing. When a guy sees tittie nipples, butt cheeks, and skin, he naturally wants to procreate. It is an instinct. We normally go with our gut feelings. Men don't like using brainpower—we are lazy. When a lady dresses provocatively, we automatically think they want to attract us sexually. Men believe at this point that women are already sexually stimulated, so it does not take much to get them in the sack. They might offer things like dinner and movies, things that are pleasing to you because they don't want to waste any time. Let's get busy! You are probably going to get the bottom of the barrel. What I mean about the bottom of the barrel is his character—don't get it confused with his assets."

Camelot stood there with one hand on her hip, and I turned toward her. "I would say a little something like this. I like the way you look in that outfit."

Camelot leaned back and said, "Thank you. I like the way you look in your outfit too," rolling her eyes over my exterior.

"My eyes are telling my mind, if you are as interesting as you look, I would never need anything else to occupy my time."

"Side note, ladies," as I look over to them, "this is what the dude's penis is telling his mind to say. What he is currently saying is exactly what he thinks he is really feeling."

Camelot stood there, and I pulled out my phone. "There is no way for me to be satisfied from this point on if I don't get your phone number. What are you doing tonight?"

"Ok, here it is. I'm free tonight."

"All he is going to think about is that booty he is going to be waxing tonight. Like I told you all before, they do not have to like but one thing about you."

"What was wrong with that? I got your attention, and you asked for my phone number," asked Camelot.

"The type of attention you got was to get screwed and nothing else."

I turned my attention to Sunshine, "Ugh... yuck... it hard to approach my BFF!"

Sunshine gave a silly grin, "We are role-playing, boy! Where are your acting skills? Put on your acting cap!"

"It is not about what I am about to say. It is my mindset. As I stepped closer to Sunshine, "Ms. Lady?"

Sunshine gave me a fleeting glance. "Hello."

"I'm pleasantly surprised to talk to a woman like you that displays such good energy."

"Why do you say that? You can tell I have good energy just by looking at me?"

"Yes, you are an authentic natural beauty, like a ray of sunshine. When the heat hits you, you know it's there."

"Well, you have overwhelmed me with the compliments, thank you."

"It is not just a compliment—it is the truth. Have you ever went shopping and looked in the window at an outfit and just knew that outfit would fit you just right?"

"Yes, I have."

"Is there any way we can exchange numbers and get to know each other better?"

"Sure, what is your number and I will call you. What time is good?"

"Ain't no time better than the present, call me now."

"Ok, Mr. Alpha male."

"I don't see her sexually. I see her intellectually."

"How can you say that? She might not scream sex in her appearance, but you don't know her intellectually because you just said two sentences to her!" Mini stated emphatically.

"Men are visual, Mini. Our vision communicates to our brain who this person is. That's why that first impression is the long-lasting impression."

Have you ever heard the term, "don't judge a book by its cover?" Mini asked.

"Unfortunately, Mini, if you saw a man in a police uniform and asked him for directions, and he said, "Don't judge a book by its cover. I ain't no police, I just like wearing this uniform.' Wouldn't that be confusing?"

"Ok, ok, ok, Ramon, but Sunshine could be the freak, and Camelot could be the nice girl, and they just dress the way they dress."

"Well, that would be great if Sunshine is the freak because it would be double the pleasure and double the fun because she has learned how to carry herself in public and in the bedroom. She would be able to reach him mentally, physically, and emotionally. That's a win-win situation for the natural girl."

I shuffled down in my seat and crossed my hands. "What I really want you to understand from this role-playing is that you need to spend more time fixing up what is on the inside than what is on the outside. Dressing provocatively and being sexy is deceptive because being sexy is a mindset, it's an attitude that has nothing to do with your clothing, how long your hair is, or the color of your lipstick and nails. That can attract men, but it cannot hold them. It is not hard for a woman to get a man with sex. What is challenging is to hold a man after sex or to get a certain caliber of man beyond sex. That's where your personality and conversation come into play. But let me give you an example, you can have a beautiful shoe box but the shoes inside can be run over with holes in the soles and this could go for your personality or sex. You can look a certain way and use your sex appeal only so far. You have to have something of substance to hold his attention. You have to have a certain approach with a man beyond sex to build a long-term relationship that ultimately leads to marriage."

"I got another role-playing scenario. Mini, come over here." Mini and I went in the back and had a huddle. I whispered in her ear the scenario we were going to play out. Mini changed into her smock and pulled the zipper down low, showing some cleavage.

We came out a few minutes later, ready for the theatrics. Everyone's eyes were on us like they were waiting for the play to start.

"Here we go, Ladies!"

Mini yelled, "Ramon!"

"I'm here," I called out.

She walked into my view and stood there posing as if she was in a sexy breast contest. I tried to ignore the rise of frustration, but my eyes were drawn to the one place that I did not want to look.

"Hey, Babe, you ready to go meet our friends for a night of bowling?"

"Yes, I'm ready," Mini said animatedly.

I was thinking *there was no way to sugar coat this*, "Ain't you going to change that blouse? I'm not comfortable with you showing that much cleavage," I said with a look of disapproval.

She halted and swung around and said, "That's a strange request to make since I was showing more cleavage when we first got together, and you didn't say anything to me then!

I stared at her with a stern expression. "This is a different situation, and our relationship has gone to another level, and you represent me now!"

"I'm grown, and you are controlling," Mini said as she walked swiftly to her station and looked at my reflection in the mirror with a frown.

I walked behind her. "I let you do it for a while, but I thought it would kick in that you would know to respect me! Why would you do something you know I don't like?!"

Mini turned to me and really got into the role and looked as if this was unbearable to her. "First of all, you are not my daddy. This is my body, and I will wear what I want when I want. Why should I change the way I dress just because you feel uncomfortable all of a sudden?!"

"Let me tell you this, I'm not your daddy, and you are not a little girl, so stop being irresponsible like one."

I stood close to Mini's face and said, "I'm trying to bring you up from being just a girlfriend to a wife. And a wife is a part of me, but I guess you can't take a girlfriend and make her a wife. Wife status has to already be in you."

"Forget You!! Why do I have to restrict the way I dress?"

"You're right. You need to go and get what you deserve! Two cannot walk together unless they agree. I guess we are unequally yoked."

Everyone started clapping uproariously! "That was so good. Y'all need a Tony award for that presentation!!" shouted Boonie.

"This role-play shows how we are addicted to bad behavior. Some women need to be validated so badly because of their insecurities that it will lead them to an alter ego that leads to vanity, that leads to self-hatred. We create this person on the outside to make us feel good on the inside. There is nothing wrong with looking good, but if you are looking good on the outside to cover up your insecurities on the inside, that's where the problem comes in."

Sweet Pea tapped her hand on the arm of her chair. "Can't you use your Hidden Secrets and still look good?"

"This does not go for everybody, just for those that display that type of behavior. If you are just as beautiful on the inside as the outside, then I am not talking to you!"

Sweet Pea raised one eyebrow in curiosity. "Well, what do you say about this? If a man breaks up with you because of how you looked and you say I'm going to go ahead and show him what he is missing. I'm going to get all cute and get my body in shape. When he sees me, he's going to wish he had me back?"

"Just because you are fine or sexy does not make you nice because beauty is only skin deep, and it is in the eye of the beholder. Nine times out of ten, a man has not broken up with you because of how you look. That's your vanity talking, not reality. It does not matter how beautiful you look. If you give a man a bitter taste about you, then that is how he will perceive you."

"If a man is just meeting a woman, how will he know what he got? If she is beautiful on the inside or not. She might be able to keep that role going for a while until they get married. That's called a pig in a blanket," Guru questioned.

"I got a saying; to shake you is to wake you! Give them the Pepsi Cola test because if you shake them up real good, whatever is in them will come out. Here is the piece of the puzzle you have been missing. When you put someone under pressure, it will reveal exactly who they are. With the test, it will not take you 6 years to understand them but rather six minutes. As for you, if your Hidden Secrets are the best thing in you, when shaken, they will come out and help you win in your relationships. That's why it is important to use them. Ladies, part of you using your Hidden Secrets is you can't always be so aggressive or blunt with what you say. You have to speak with an air of femininity and softness sometimes. When a man sees a woman as a wife, she has a much more subtle way about her. She is more conservative in her appearance, attractive, pulled together but not in an overblown sleazy way. You say I like stilettos and wearing makeup, and that is fine, but know how to accentuate what you have in a classy way, and you will do much better in the fish you catch."

Mini got up from her chair and moved closer to me, made eye contact, and sat down at one of the stations next to me. "Ramon, can you clear this up for me? This is something I have been wondering about for a while. For instance, when I go to the grocery store, I will have on my sweats, gym shoes, no weave, and no makeup and get tons of attention from men. When I have my weave freshly done, makeup, and my best shoes and clothes on, I don't get half the attention from men. Why not?"

I looked directly into her eyes. "When you are natural, men are drawn to you because it radiates something authentic and real and not synthetic. He can detect that you don't have walls and barriers up. He can see your natural essence, and that is more attractive. When you dress to the nines, he notices your alter ego. Your alter ego is not the real you. Therefore, it is difficult for a man to identify and connect with you. That is one reason he will misjudge or misinterpret you. He might think you are bourgeois or a slut, and you could be none of those things."

Suddenly, I got up from my chair and paced to the middle of the floor with a smile and said, "Women need to know their true beauty. Let me explain what true beauty is. It is inside of you. Beauty is appealing to the senses. It's not your looks but your outlook that dictates your outcome. It's as simple as seeing his vision and pushing him through it, protecting your ear gate to hearing no evil, the aroma of a home-cooked meal, the gentle stroke of his ego, and the sweet taste of your good attitude. Do you want him to see your inner beauty or your booty? However, they see your beauty on the inside, that's how they will view you on the outside."

CHAPTER 10

— ❧ —

Pot of Gold

After you read this book and apply the principles and precepts the pot of gold at the end of your rainbow is here. You are that pot of gold, and now you understand the pot of gold is within you.

"HEY, WE HAVE talked about a lot of stuff, but we have not talked about the elephant in the room that usually breaks up relationships; finances," Mini stated.

"We can talk about finances, but you have something worth more than money, and that is gold. You are the gold, and you are the most precious thing in the world. You are the most important thing in a relationship, not money. Money can be a stumbling block in a relationship if you don't know how to use your Hidden Secrets. We know the love of money is the root of all evil, but love of each other will overcome evil. You conquer evil with good."

"Let's get these money questions going. Who wants to ask the first question?"

"Ramon, this is something women say all the time, a couple that was living together had a problem with their joint account. Her guy did not like the fact that she would spend her money on shoes, purses, or whatever she wanted every week without concern toward their mutual budget. She said she contributes her hard-earned money and therefore should be able to spend it on whatever she likes without him questioning her about it. What do you think?" Boonie asked.

I walked to the window, and the sun had begun to issue an introduction of its arrival as the rain slowed down. "She should have looked at what he said and honored it. When their household bills were a shared responsibility, then she should have been considerate of that. Maybe he was trying to build up a nest egg. Obviously, there was a lack of communication there. She didn't understand that. She sounded plain selfish. If she did not want to share her "hard-earned" money, then she should have never moved in with him and started a joint account. She was spending money every week. Not only was she spending hers, but his too."

As I walked back from the window toward Boonie, folding my arms, I continued. "If she cannot respect what he says, then she needs to be by herself. When she made a selfish statement like that about their finances, that shut down all communication. Now, he just wants to defend his honor because she's not respecting his wishes. This is something you have to understand about men."

"I'm next!" said Sunshine. "My question is really good!! We want to know if a woman has an apartment that is $2700 a month and her guy has an apartment that's $850 a month, but his apartment is in an unsafe environment, but they have been discussing moving in with each other. He wants her to come live at his place because it is more economical. She refuses because she feels safer where she stays. What should they do?"

I answered her question while Sunshine stared at her notes with a pen poised, ready to write. "Women are naturally the nesters in the relationship. It is very important to a woman where she lives. This is a situation that calls for compromise.

He should give her more leeway in order for her to flow in her full capacity, which is the nurturer. She has to feel comfortable in order to bring him comfort. Men should always let women pick the living arrangements. Remember when we discussed that a woman will take a house and make it a home? This is the same principle. The compromise would be for him to give her a price range and let her pick it out. A place she feels safe in and loves to call home. This will make for a more harmonious living arrangement."

Camelot made a remark as she looked at her nails, "This is not 'no problem.' The problem would be if they could not afford the rent!"

I walked over to Camelot, and we touched fingertips, "You right about that!"

Guru shook her head and asked, "Ramon, what would you do if you move into a house with a female and you and the female both work. You tell her you expect her to pay half of the bills. She tells you no, you are the provider, and you should pay all the bills?"

"How old is this chick? She sounds dated," Mini asked in surprise.

"Man, she must be a widow or something or 77 years old for her to think like this!" Camelot responded.

Guru explained, "I'm not sure how old she is but this is a question some women can relate to no matter what age!"

"What woman in this day in age would be asking this of any man unless he is ballin'?" Sunshine commented. "She sounds like a gold digger to me!"

I chuckled. "Are y'all finished talking about the lady like a dog? My answer to this would be: in the bible, it says the man is supposed to be the provider and some women stand on it for their own special benefits. If you say he is the provider, then you need to quit your job and let him be the provider. A man is a provider on many levels, not just money. He provides love, protection, and ministry. But if you are making money, then it is to better both of your lives, not just yours. If you quit your job, you should be able to help him to reach his goals. If you can't do it that way, then take the money you make and help him reach it another way with your finances. If you can't do that, you don't need to be a wife; stay a girlfriend because a wife is a good thing, not a burden."

"What is she supposed to do with her money, spend it on herself? She sounds selfish," Sunshine commented.

"At one time, I was thinking like that. Everybody likes a sponsor," Sweet Pea added. "I know better now, and my relationship means more than money. You can't go in a plural relationship thinking singular; you eventually will end up singular. Take it from me, I've been there."

I nodded my head in affirmation. "That was a great answer, Sweet Pea."

Boonie folded her arms. "So many of my clients and friends say that men these days don't like to spend any money, they don't take them nowhere, they don't buy them nothing. How do you get a man to spend money on you is the question?"

"That is a very superficial question, and if that is what they are looking for, they need to put a hoe uniform on. That makes men want to procreate and let them know it costs. They will only shortchange themselves because what I've been telling you is how to get his mind, body, and soul with your power of persuasion. With your Hidden Secrets, everything comes with that package."

I maneuver between Sweet Pea and Boonie's chair, so everyone could see me better. "You have to take these tools and make them practical. If you want to go out to dinner, maybe you need to cook dinner. If you want a man to call you before midnight, you need to have something to talk about. If you want somebody to buy you something, then you need to make yourself available to meet his needs. What I mean by needs is, what are his dreams, his goals, his endeavors, and how you can play a part in making those things happen?"

Sunshine added, "This is my take on it. You are going to have to put yourself out there and be vulnerable, unselfish, and trustworthy, and that takes heart and courage. You will have to take a chance on another person. If you are not willing to take the risk, then you won't have him the way you want him."

Mini looked in the mirror with an expression of resolution. "We hear what you are saying, but when I was in a relationship, it was not easy to allow myself to be open. I had to guard my heart. My defense mechanism automatically came up. Now, after listening to you, I was operating in fear, and that can never work in a relationship. I used to believe that if he wanted me enough, he would be willing to go through the walls or hell and high water to get the prize, which was me. Then, and only then, would I be willing to let my guard down."

"Let me reiterate where I think you are going with this. When a man pursues you, they are automatically conquerors; they will continue to push through obstacles you might put in their way to achieve their goal. But don't be fooled—their goal may be just to have sex with you, and after that, there is nothing else for them to achieve or conquer. Remember, they only have to like one thing about you, but if they're busy trying to give you what you want, who is fulfilling their needs?"

I leaned back on my station and crossed my arms. "The flip side to this is that men understand when you put walls and barriers up, that means you have a lot of battle scars, and you have been put through the wringer. One of the detections to let them know this is the walls and barriers. A woman that is pure and decent is not going to have any defense mechanisms up because she has not been through all of those battles. Therefore, she will be able to tap into her man easier because she is more willing to be open to see who he is. In a nutshell, this is about planting a good seed and watering it with faith. If you are afraid, to move forward in courage, you have to become a new person."

"What do you mean by pure and decent?" Boonie asked

"Let me define it for you in the context of what I have been talking about. If you are in fear, that is what causes a defense mechanism. This is what causes you to think wrong about a person in your heart. That diminishes your ability to be pure of heart. You are incapable of being decent if you put up a wall of defense. You are treating me as if I am on the opposing team. You come off as hostile, which is the opposite of pure and decent.

"You have to operate in faith. Ain't that right, Great One?" Camelot said.

"You are right, Camelot," I said.

"Hypothetically speaking, we know the answer but..." as Sweet Pea looked pointedly at me, "we want to know what you have to say. This lady is in a relationship with a guy, and she is not attracted to him sexually, plus she doesn't like his look. He takes care of her financially. He has asked her to marry him. Should she marry him for security and try to learn to love him?"

"If you're willing to pay the price, then go for it because there's always a price to pay. If being secure means that much to you, and you are willing to make a sacrifice of love, companionship, or intimacy, then it will be a hole in your life that cannot be fulfilled. Your reasons for marriage should not be for physical attraction and money—it should be for love. Physical looks and money can change, but love is eternal! This is something my grandmother used to always say: the grass may be greener on the other side, but I guarantee you, it's a higher water bill."

"Well, your grandmother was a wise woman. But if the water bill is higher, at least with enough money, I can pay it," Camelot intervened.

"It can be paid, but you are going to make a sacrifice, and if you are willing to do it, you are all good!"

"Here's another question, Great One." Guru hesitated like she was trying to decide if it was a good question. "My client said she and her child moved in with her man, and she feels that it's his responsibility to cover all her child's expenses. He says he's not going to do it. Let his father do it. She told him, 'if you don't want to provide for my child, and if you don't take us as a package deal, I am leaving.' She was asking me should she leave?"

"My answer to your client would be this: It's a package, no doubt, and if he cares for you, he should understand that. But he is not the biological father, so there is probably going to be a difference. The difference is he should be a contributing factor on his own terms, depending on how he and the child get along. They would have to connect like father and child, and he may not be willing to go that far, and if not, you have to be willing to take up the slack."

"I'm a part of this women-only site on my social media, and this is a question that the members always ask over and over, if a man loses his job, should you help him financially?" Mini asked.

"Yes, you should help him, that's why you're considered a helpmate."

"Well, some women would think if you help him, it will make him lose his incentive, and he'll just lay on the couch and not do nothing."

"If you are not using your power of persuasion to lift him off the couch and make him believe that he can move a mountain when he is around you, then that must be the negative energy you are giving him. Why are you giving him that energy, and why do you think less of him? Why are you planting negative seeds? You must want to keep him on the couch, so you can feel good about yourself. If that's not true, you would be motivating him to do what he needs to do."

Sunshine emerged back from the bathroom and jumped into the conversation, "Mini, you need to stay off those women-only sites!"

Mini gave Sunshine a puzzled look, "Why, what is wrong with them?"

"How can a bunch of angry, man-hating women, who don't have no man, don't know how to keep one, give you advice? That's like the blind leading the blind. They do not have your best interest at heart. They just want to make you as miserable and lonely as they are. I have been on those sites, and those women sound crazy to me. They ask questions that any woman with any sense of self would know the answer to."

"Well, after today, I don't plan on being on there anymore. I just gave some questions that were on the site."

I quickly asked, "Do you have any more questions from that site?"

"Ramon, you wouldn't believe how many questions," Mini said as she twisted her lip up.

"Well, let's have a few more. That way, if you decide to go back on there, you can give them some good advice."

Mini pondered. "Umm… here's another one. If y'all bought everything together and y'all had a breakup, and they wanted most of the furniture, but y'all bought it together, what do you do?"

"You have to weigh your options. Are your peace and your sanity worth more than material things? If so, you may have to make a sacrifice. What is greater; peace of mind or a bunch of controversies?"

"Ramon, that was a sweet answer, but that buster is gonna have to give me my stuff!" Boonie said.

"This is not to make you feel like a failure or put you down. You do not need to be perfect. Sometimes, you're not just going to be able to execute what you learned right away. I don't expect you to, but this is a guide to help you along the way. It's going to take some conditioning and practice to get to that level. So, I understand how you feel, but at least you have a start"

"These are tools in your arsenal of life to help you be the pot of gold."

Mini looked at her phone. "Here is another question: your man doesn't make much money, and he wants to take you to a cheaper restaurant, and you want to go somewhere more expensive, and you are willing to pay for it, do you give him the money beforehand, so as to not make him feel bad or do you just pay for it outright?"

"Well, actually, you can put some money in a nice card, and right before y'all go out, give him the card. That way, you don't have to worry about it anymore. Just note for future reference if there is a problem with something as little as this that there will probably be more problems down the road when it comes to money."

Guru said, "This is what I think. You might have more expensive taste and make more money than him, and you want to share different experiences, and you feel he deserves it, and you don't mind spending the money on him. Hopefully, he would not feel intimidated by you paying for it."

"Based on what Ramon has been teaching us today, maybe I might say it's my treat, but other times you might not want to bruise his ego, and you would need to do something that is within his means. For example, he brings you daisies, and you prefer Oceana roses, but he can only afford the daisies. You do not go out and buy yourself roses and say it is from him, but you make him think those daisies are the best thing ever. Ain't that right, Great One?" Mini stated.

"Yeah, something like that!"

Mini studied all her notes and put her pen down, and said, "Here's another one. Why do men ask you silly questions like can I stay with you? Would you buy me a phone? Put me on your credit card? Or will you cosign for me to get a car?"

"Many times men do that because it has worked before. Women will do certain things for men for leverage, so they can get their hooks in them and have control over that particular situation because it's important when a woman is insecure to control the situation. You can't have a healthy relationship trying to control someone with things."

"I would have to understand how he functions to put him on my credit," Sweet Pea said.

Mini said, "Here are a series of questions from the site. If you are married, who should be in charge of the finances?"

"Whoever is the most proficient in budgeting."

"Why does a man feel so intimidated because a woman makes more money than him?"

"A man is not intimidated by a woman that makes more money than him unless she is using her money to make him feel inadequate." The ladies looked up from their pads with a sideways glance as I continued. "You are a helpmate; why would a man be resistant to that? It goes back to what I have said—it is how you make him feel when he is with you. It has something to do with your personality, not him."

"Wait a minute, Ramon. Men sometimes come into a relationship with an inferiority complex of their own that has nothing to do with a female's personality, and that makes them be intimidated by a successful woman that might make more money than they do," Mini said.

"Sometimes men are insecure, and they do use their money to get what they want. They might want just one thing from you, and if they find out you have more money than them, they can't use finances to make you do what they want you to do. He might leave you when he sees he can't control you in the way he wants to because you already have money. What you would need to do in this instance is use your Hidden Secrets to get to the bottom of his insecurities and help him to work it out where his ego stays intact."

"If you are in a relationship with a person who spends his money frivolously and you don't, should you withdraw your money from the joint account and set up a separate account?" Boonie asked.

"Maybe you need to try to guide and coach him in how to do better with his money. If that doesn't work, then yes, you should separate your money because he sounds foolish, and the bible says a fool and his money are soon parted."

I glanced over at the window and could see it was still drizzling and the sun was peeking out the clouds. "Living together separately, even with your finances, can lead to you both outgrowing each other. Pooling your finances helps you to grow and stay together. When you both have your money tied up, you will be a little more cautious about what you do outside of the relationship."

"Ramon, you're right to tell them to separate their money because if that fool spent all my money, and I can't buy me a pair of panties, then that sucker would be in the wind. Baby Bye!" Camelot said with fervor.

"I love to shop, and I use to hide merchandise from my significant other to keep the peace. Was that wrong?" Sweet Pea questioned.

"Yes, that was wrong. Being slick comes in different forms, so when it comes back your way, do not be mad. Try not to be slick about anything, including finances. People come through the door incorrect but expect others to be correct. Don't make money your God. Money has a life of its own. Do not let money overtake you."

"You are right, and I understand what you are saying, but I'm a shopaholic, so what's wrong with trying to keep the peace?" Sweet Pea asked.

"Ain't no right way to do wrong!"

"This has truly been a day to remember. I'm proud of you all. If you didn't learn anything today, please be mindful that you have to fix yourself before you can help fix someone else. When you look in the mirror, and you have done that, then you have just changed the universe. Everybody is looking for coal mines. That's where you find coal, that's where you find something valuable, and we know a diamond is just a lump of coal that knows how to handle the pressure. The more pressure you put on it, the more it shines."

I continued. "You ladies are diamond and gold all put together."

I looked at each of the ladies, and all their eyes went soft.

"Let's see what you ladies have learned so far. Mini, can you find some more non-finance questions on the site?"

"Sure, no problem," Mini said.

"I want each of you to tell me what your answer will be to these questions based on what you have learned."

The girls started shuffling through their notes without even looking up.

"Here is my first non-financial question from the site. How can a man be with a woman for eight years, break up with her, and then after a year, marry another woman?" Mini asked.

I squinted my eyes as if doing so would allow me to see them better. "I want one of you ladies to answer that question."

Boonie crossed her arm, put one hand under her chin as if thinking especially hard, and spoke. "From what I've learned, a man can love you if you give him what he desires. You can be all the things he wants and be missing that one ingredient that he needs. Before today's discussion, I would have been thinking that he was stringing her along. It would have sound hurtful knowing he wasn't going to marry her.

I answered. "You're right. For instance, women do this a thousand times more than men. Ask your friends or yourself how many of your boyfriends have asked to marry you but you all said no."

"Well, I've had at least five proposals, so you are correct. I knew I wasn't going to marry them. They had some issues I don't even want to talk about, and I was not willing to deal with all that. Even though I loved them, we eventually fell out," Sweet Pea added.

"It is vice versa for a man, and Boonie was right. You can give him what he desires, and he can love some things about you but you can be missing that one ingredient he requires."

"We women will sometimes use a double standard. When men do this type of thing to us, we call it hurtful, but if we do it to a man, we call it protecting ourselves. But now we better understand we cannot have it both ways," Guru said.

"That's why you must use your Hidden Secrets and tap into him to know what he needs," I answered.

Mini explained, "This is not a question, but one of the ladies made this comment. She said she went through her God-sent husband's phone and social media. He found out and got angry and divorced her. The other members on the site responded and said he wasn't God-sent because if he was, no matter what you did to him, he wouldn't have left you."

"It would seem he divorced her for more than that!" Sunshine said with emphasis.

Authoritatively speaking, I said, "It was more than that—it was a mindset. She is operating in fear. If she doesn't find a problem in the wash, she will find it in the rinse."

"When God put something together, and it was meant to be, wouldn't it be?" Sweet Pea asked.

"She was operating in fear instead of faith. You cannot put light and darkness in the same place. Am I right?" Mini asked.

A long silence hung in the air.

"We got everything you have been saying, but this comment is a little bit over our head. What would you say to this?" Camelot responded.

"Mini was right, but let me elaborate on it. A lot of times, people say what's meant to be will be, but that's not true. Faith is not by chance. God can bless you with a husband, but if you don't operate in faith, then you are operating in fear. Her fellow site members were giving her advice out of pure chance. God has nothing to do with chance; He is not a gambler. Your marriage is not like rolling the dice and letting the chips fall where they may. The marriage must flow in faith, and if you believe that your husband is God-sent, then there is no way you should not believe in him and be sneaking around in his things. Even if you all had a misunderstanding three or four times, you have to believe in faith that you can move that mountain and it will move, that's faith. If you are having massive problems repeatedly, you have to have faith that it's going to work out until you turn that thing around and not by chance."

"Ah, Ramon, that was very enlightening!" Camelot exclaimed as the group seemed to nod in agreement.

"Yeah, I'm glad you distinguished between chance and faith because I used to say if it didn't work out, it was not meant to be." Guru stood up and raised her hands. "But I used to think that was faith, but it wasn't, it was by chance. Faith needs to be activated. I need to work on that!"

Sunshine raised up high in her chair and extolled. "Man, you are preaching to the choir. In my 20-plus years of marriage,

I have had to use my faith many times, and God has not failed me yet. There were many challenges. I had to walk in faith, apply my faith, and God turned it around. It was not always easy. I did not know how it would turn out, but God did it and not at all by chance!"

Sweet Pea shouted, "Won't He do it!"

Everyone gave a glorious response. "Yes, He will!"

I was thinking to myself, *I want my narratives to help them understand not only the depth of love but also the great power inside of them*. I strolled around the salon and paused and said with a long sigh, "Here is another scenario for you all to show what y'all know now! One day, one of my faithful clients came to me for advice regarding her marriage. She started to tell me that she had found her husband of 7 years in their bed with another woman. She was devastated and broken by this. She felt they were in a good place after 7 years of marriage and was so confused by why he would do such a thing to hurt her so. She asked me what she should do?"

Sweet Pea shuffled her notes around and said, "Based on what I have learned, this is what I would do. After I have had time to calm down, then first find out why he did it. He tells me why, then I would tell him, "I forgive you, and for whatever reason you have done this, I know this was not your character. You are a decent and honorable man, and that's why I forgive you. Because I know you did not mean to do this.' Now he is in my debt. Is that not correct Ramon?"

I nodded yes.

"This is what I told my faithful client about how to win back her husband. First of all, I asked her, 'Do you love him?' She said, 'Yes.' Real love covers a multitude of imperfections. You have to forgive him wholeheartedly. You can never bring it back up. If you do bring it back up, you are not operating in total faith and forgiveness. You have to operate in faith. Whatever you want, he will give you. What is that you want? It does not have to be gold, silver, or money because some things mean more than that. It can be attention or whatever you realize you need. He will be willing to give it to you. I want you to know when someone invests in you, they take a special interest in you. They become more concerned with their investment. It brings about a new level of commitment. It's not about the money, but to help him remember you are a pot of gold and how valuable you are in personality alone. You are his refuge. Wherever a man's money is, that's where his heart is. He is willing to pay that debt in so many ways. So, when he's paying it off, he becomes deeply involved in you. Now here's the double dose of the megaplex. When you have him wide open, start planting good seeds in him by being submissive. We know that being submissive is one of your powers. Then follow it up with your power of persuasion; he will jump off a building for you now. If you tell him how dirty he is, you can be sure he will not praise you for that. Or better yet, you can show him the goodness in you, and he will love you more for that. Once you think of him in the most beautiful way, he must adore you for believing in him."

I opened my drawer, placing my combs in their proper place. "This is how you win, ladies! Sometimes, no pain, no gain. Sometimes, you have to make a sacrifice and put your emotions to the side for a minute in order to make things better. None of this will happen by chance! This happens by being committed. Then this is when you get the results you always wanted. Like the bible says, 'What the devil meant for evil, God can turn it around for your good!"

"That's real faith right there. I already know the outcome of this!" Guru said.

"Of course, she did exactly what I told her. I did not hear back from her for a few months, but when she did contact me, she was very excited to share the outcome. She told me they moved to a new house, he got a transfer from his job to a new location. She said he is really focused on her, and it's like their relationship has a new life."

"Man, that sounds almost too good to be true. I can't wait to get out of here because I'm going to use my Hidden Secrets today!" Sweet Pea declared.

Mini said, "I have a new-found outlook on relationships. I know I have been extremely critical of men, and that can only perpetuate negativity in the relationship. Whatever the situation is, even when it is bad, you have to turn that thing around with your power of persuasion." She cocked her head to one side. "Ramon, you got to give it to a sister—I'm I right or I'm I right?" You have to know how to put your emotions to the side to the betterment of your relationship. That's where I have been making my mistakes."

"You are so right, my sister, but you have to understand logic and emotion are two different things. This is something that takes time, don't worry, you will be fine."

As I looked out the window and saw the rain had stopped and the sun had come out and dissolved the shadows in the salon.

Guru opened her notebook. "This is what I have in some of my notes; being good is not just walking around doing good things for people. It's being able to be challenged and be victorious in those challenges through faith and righteousness. In order to be a good woman, companion, or wife, you have to be able to deal with difficulties in a good way."

Sunshine gave a huge smile in Guru's direction. "Girl, what kind of notes have you been taking? I'm really impressed, that was very good!"

Guru batted her eyes as she peeked over her notebook, "What can I say?" Everyone laughed.

"This has been an excellent session. Believe it or not, I have learned a lot just by listening to you all. But you can be sure people always make excuses for their problems. We women have to understand problems are to be fixed. God made a woman for a man to solve an equation." As Sunshine organized her station, "Women are problem solvers in a relationship and whatever those problems might be for a man such as loneliness, need for encouragement, organization, assistance in life choices, you have the power to fix it. The best way to do this is to lead by example. That is why we are considered a pot of gold because men know how valuable we really are."

"I did not make it 20 years without being a pot of gold baby!" Sunshine said with a sassy expression.

"Shut up, girl, before we take this blow dryer and give you a blow out!" Boonie said in fun.

"Ramon, I feel like this; if what you say can't help me, I can't be helped because you are telling the truth and nothing but the truth. Just thinking about listening to people singing love yourself. No, sometimes we love ourselves too much! Oh my God, the world has gotten so backward and topsy-turvy about how to deal with relationship situations." Camelot continued with heightened emotions. "What you taught us about tapping into a man has been a revelation for me. Men have a certain language, and you have to understand that language, so you can counter their actions."

Boonie made a compelling comment. "We need to start turning the tides, and one way is to stop being so loyal to our flesh. Let's learn to be more selfless and let our flesh die daily, so our spirits can be willing. Hidden Secrets lets our mind conform to a new mindset. This is not only a spiritual conversation, but it is factual. This is one area that I noted and has captivated me."

The sun came out, and the light glazed the room. "What you learned today, take it with you and use it." I looked at the clock and saw the time was winding down. "You're able to come up against the worst challenges and overcome them because in life, you're going to come up against some difficult times, but it's being able to see them through. Take them and turn them around and conquer them. This is how you win."

Sweet Pea walked toward the reception desk and turned halfway around. "Nothing is problem proof, but I look at problems differently. Now, whatever I'm challenged with, I know how to lay back and understand how that person functions and don't panic when I'm hit with an issue because I got the antidote for the disease. Studying my notes is the prescription. Hello!" She turned and kept walking with a strut.

Guru placed her curling iron in the curl rack. "You're on the money with that. I need to practice not getting emotional. I'm going to stay ready every day of my life, learning how to take a deep breath and stay cool." She made her point with a comb suspended in her hand.

Mini swung her hips as she swayed them side to side. "I'm staying in my femininity. I can't lose in my natural state of beauty. Let me be challenged, but I will come out victorious!" she said, rotating her right thigh and hip. "In life, people get hurt. That's life. We have all been hurt before, so what you do? You shed some light on the blind, you feed the hungry with knowledge, you give the hopeless hope. And for heartbreak?" She looked at me and nodded her head. "You have to give that time!"

As the sun rays streamed through the window, no longer hidden by the clouds, we all started packing up our stations, getting ready to call it a day as they gathered their notes together and took their smocks off. I looked up and meaningfully said, "Girls, please don't lose those notes—they're valuable!

They all rolled their heads up and down with a nod. "We won't do that. This is our lifeline on relationships," Guru confirmed.

Camelot walked to the window to close the blinds. "Look, y'all, there's a rainbow in the sky."

We all went to the window and looked. Everybody chatted about how beautiful it was.

I explained, "Whenever you see a rainbow, that is God's covenant that He will never destroy the earth again with a flood. No matter how much it rains, the rain will eventually stop, and the sun will shine again. The saying is that at the end of every rainbow is a pot of gold, and that's you!"

"Ramon, that's so sweet. Thank you for this beautiful session. This was meant to happen," Guru said, hugging me goodbye.

As each gathered their things and whisked out the door, I got ready to leave. I looked around and thought to myself, *this was needed. Thank you God. What a perfect day to plant good seeds in rich soil* as I clicked the lights off and walked out the door.

Summary

THIS IS A self-help book with a twist, something different. I hope this book has been a blessing to you, the reader. It has been an honor to share my experiences from different walks of life when it comes to women and men with you. The purpose of this book is to take you from a bad space and put you in a good place. Do not be dismayed when these concepts don't happen right away; you have to practice and condition yourself. Don't feel bad if you don't get it right the first time; you have to have faith. Faith to continue to do it until you get it.

Problems won't be solved in a day. In life, you must have patience. Patience is a very important element in the success of these concepts, without it, they cannot be done. It is my prayer that I have brought you to some level of understanding on how to win in relationships. Everyone has some good in them but there is a difference between being good and just existing. These Hidden Secrets that I revealed have to be activated daily to a point you can recognize them and use them to your advantage. Whatever you face in relationships, know that there is no situation that is so big you cannot overcome it. There is always hope at the end of the rainbow.

The strongest thing is not always the skill but the will!

Now that you've read the book, I'm curious what your thoughts are.

Did the book change the way you think about the dynamics between women and men?

_____

_____

_____

_____

_____

What did you most relate to?

_____

_____

_____

_____

_____

Would knowing this (answer from previous question) have changed how you reacted to a situation?

_____

_____

_____

_____

_____

How would it have affected the end-result of your situation if you had used your Hidden Secrets?

_____

_____

_____

_____

_____

If you have questions for me, please contact me at www.myhiddensecrets.com. I would love to hear from you!

Also by Ramon Darnell: *Human Earthquake Book 1 Available on Amazon.com.*

For questions or press inquiries, please contact the author at

708-730-4664

humanearthquake123@gmail. com